D0871033

# Blue Ridge

Alison Gieschen

iUniverse, Inc.
Bloomington

# BLUE RIDGE

*Copyright © 2013 Alison Gieschen.*

*All rights reserved. No part of this book may be used or reproduced by any means, graphic, electronic, or mechanical, including photocopying, recording, taping or by any information storage retrieval system without the written permission of the publisher except in the case of brief quotations embodied in critical articles and reviews.*

*iUniverse books may be ordered through booksellers or by contacting:*

*iUniverse*
*1663 Liberty Drive*
*Bloomington, IN 47403*
*www.iuniverse.com*
*1-800-Authors (1-800-288-4677)*

*Because of the dynamic nature of the Internet, any web addresses or links contained in this book may have changed since publication and may no longer be valid. The views expressed in this work are solely those of the author and do not necessarily reflect the views of the publisher, and the publisher hereby disclaims any responsibility for them.*

*Any people depicted in stock imagery provided by Thinkstock are models, and such images are being used for illustrative purposes only.*

*Certain stock imagery © Thinkstock.*

*ISBN: 978-1-4759-7744-8 (sc)*
*ISBN: 978-1-4759-7746-2 (hc)*
*ISBN: 978-1-4759-7745-5 (e)*

*Library of Congress Control Number: 2013903310*

*Printed in the United States of America*

*iUniverse rev. date: 3/21/2013*

# Dedication

THIS BOOK IS DEDICATED TO my mother, who believed in me and gave me the inspiration to write; to my husband, who loves and supports me in every possible way; to my children, who are the lights of my life; and to my friends, who know how crazy my life is but are still willing to be my friends.

# *Prologue*

LAURA COULD SMELL THE ALCOHOL on her father's breath from her hiding spot in the corner of the room. Her body trembled as she huddled against the wall in the corner. She sat with her legs tucked up tightly against her chest, arms crossed around them. She rocked back and forth slightly, feeling the sickening anticipation of what was about to unfold. First, there had been yelling—her father screaming at her mother for things that were beyond her control. Then came the crashing of beer bottles thrown across the room shattering against the walls. When her father went on his drunken rampages, Laura knew to make herself disappear. She had tried once or twice to intervene on her mother's behalf, but that always ended with her being beaten up, bruised, and battered. Her mother took the abuse regularly and always warned Laura to stay away when Father got angry. Just recently, the rampages had gotten worse, and Laura's worst fears were about to come true.

"I done told you a thousand times you need to clean up this pigsty," her father bellowed drunkenly at her mother. *Crash*. A beer bottle exploded, and Laura's mother screamed. "I'm gonna teach you a lesson good this time. Don't say I didn't warn ya."

The only light in the room came from a dim bulb hanging from the center of the ceiling and a few flickering candles Laura had lit earlier in the evening—enough light to see her mother backing into the bedroom and trying to close the door against the weight of her drunken father, who stood over six feet tall and weighed a good two hundred pounds. Laura's slim mother had no chance to defend herself against his rage. Laura rocked and glanced, her eyes fixed in a glassy stare, seeing but not wanting to see, as her father muscled his way into the doorway. Laura's last glimpse of her mother was her angelic face, contorted in suffering, her mousy brown hair hanging in wet strings down her forehead and across her face, tears streaming down her face. Her father pushed his way into the room, flinging the door violently against the wall behind it. She watched in horror as her father drew his arm back and then sent it forward, delivering a stinging slap across her mother's face that sent her flying backward onto the bed. There were sounds of a struggle, a few muffled screams, and then Laura watched as her mother's arm dangled down beside the bed. It hung, ashy and twisted, in an unnatural direction. It twitched once and then was still.

Somehow, Laura understood that was the last time she was going to see her mother. Without her mother, she knew her life would be in danger from her drunken, worthless father. Struggling to hold back her tears, she crawled on her hands and knees toward the doorway. The wooden floor was gritty beneath her hands and knees, and she ignored the splinters breaking off into her hands. Her only goal was to get to the door. "One step at a time," her momma used to tell her, and now her life depended on those very words. Her father seemed quiet in the bedroom, but Laura did not want to chance arousing him. She quietly crept across the room to the front door and rose up on her knees to open the latch. She felt the cool air drifting under and around the gaps in the doorframe. The latch protested and then finally opened with a grinding sound and a loud click.

"Where the hell do you think you're going!" roared her father from the bedroom.

Laura's flight instincts immediately took over. She stood, threw open the door, and bolted into the night, barefoot, wearing only a nightgown and a robe. Vicious barking attacked her senses as she ran past the kennel. She halted, knowing her father was too drunk to follow her quickly, and she took a moment to open the kennel and grab the dog. Better to have the dog as an ally than to leave him to help track her scent for her father. As she turned to bolt into the forest behind her home, she abruptly kicked something hard. She stumbled and fell to the ground. The earth smelled mossy, like decaying leaves and moist soil, and she focused on its comforting scent rather than the pain shooting into the shin that had collided with the mystery object. Feeling behind her to find the source of the impact, her hand found and traced the metal shape. It was hard and rusty and had a spout and a handle—a gas can.

# *Chapter 1*

LAURA BREATHED SHALLOW, QUICK, RAGGED breaths; her eyes darted back and forth beneath her closed lids. Suddenly, she woke with a gasp and bolted upright in bed, breathing heavily. She sat up and flung the covers to the side. Swinging her legs over the edge of the bed, she cradled her head in her hands, taking deep breaths, trying to stop the shaky feeling left over from the nightmare. Twelve years had passed since she had lost her mother, but she still missed her desperately. The memory of that terrible night often haunted her in her sleep. She opened her eyes and looked around the bedroom. Soft light filtered through the floor-to-ceiling windows decorated with tan and brown curtains. A fifty-two-inch flat-screen television hung above the white marble fireplace across the room from her bed. Textured beige carpet covered the floor of the bedroom, contrasting the dark, polished bedroom furniture. As a child, she'd been lucky to have one pillow; now a stack of six decorative pillows lay on the floor next to her bed, which was covered with a thick, soft cream-colored quilt. Slipping off the bed into her sheepskin slippers, she drifted in a sleepy haze over to the window to bathe herself in the new morning light. Gently, she pressed her hand against the cold glass to give herself a shocking reminder that her life was not a dream. It was indeed a reality, although Laura would not have been surprised to wake up at any moment and find herself back in the shabby apartment that had been her home one year ago. Staring out the window from her second-story perch, Laura struggled with reality. *Okay, I am Mrs. Laura McBane. I live in this beautiful townhouse in Asheville, North Carolina. That is my black BMW parked in the driveway below.* Laura pulled her hand away from the window, backed up a few steps, and then turned and sprinted back toward the bed. Giggling wildly, she threw herself down on the bed and covered her face with her pillow. Her laughter faded into sobs, a few sighs, and then a calm stillness. Why did her life seem so unreal? Why couldn't she accept that fate had finally dealt her a decent hand? Couldn't a person shed the past, stop looking behind them, and live on for the future? There was no question she would try. Would she succeed?

Rising out of her analysis of her tremulous emotions, Laura kicked off her slippers and walked to her bathroom. The white Italian tile felt cold to her feet after the softness of her bedroom carpet. The bathroom was bright from the sun beaming through the glass panels in the ceiling. The marble vanity had two sinks; hers was to the right. She automatically went to her side and pulled open the solid oak drawer to get her toothbrush and toothpaste. Jim insisted that nothing be left on the counter. Everything had to be stowed neatly in the drawers, the countertops shined before she left in the morning. As she brushed her teeth she stared at the vases on the windowsill. There were gold-plated, intricate patterns weaved into their texture. They'd been here long before she arrived, and she guessed they were quite expensive. She removed her silk night garments and placed them neatly on the edge of the Jacuzzi tub. She stepped across the cold tiles into the large raised, all-glass shower stall and started the hot water. The steam from the hot water quickly clouded the cubicle. As she stepped into the shower, the steam offered little protection from the strange perception she had of being totally exposed, like a piece of artwork on a pedestal in a glass case. Having dealt with a lifetime of low self-esteem, Laura couldn't describe this feeling of vulnerability she often experienced to Jim. Her body was the only possession that remained from her former life—a life that focused on survival, not on enjoyment of physical beauty.

After three months of marriage, Laura still managed to take her morning showers after Jim had gone downstairs or left for work so that she could be alone. She wondered if there would ever be a time when she would stand in the shower, totally unconscious of her nakedness, while her husband performed his morning shaving rituals. With that thought still on her mind, she quickly finished showering, too preoccupied to languish under the soothing warm water. After wringing the excess water out of her long, wet locks, she stepped out of the shower and wrapped herself in the oversized soft cotton towel. Fighting off the overwhelming nagging feeling that she should be in a hurry to be somewhere, she went back into the bedroom and picked out black stretch pants and a blue floral athletic top. She got dressed and returned to the bathroom to quickly dry her hair. She pulled it up into a ponytail and then moisturized her face and put on some eyeliner and mascara. Jim liked the natural look and strictly forbade her to wear much makeup except on the most formal occasions.

As Laura drove to the gym, she was reminded of the first time she met her husband. Laura had seen Jim several times at the club where they were both members. At first, Jim just watched her from a distance. She noticed many men watching her when she exercised, but Jim was the most intense. Many of the single women had joined the club with the hope they would meet an attractive, muscular hunk. Laura was one of the few single women who joined simply to keep herself in shape. She was tall and slender, with an above-average build, but she worked hard to stay in shape. Sheepishly, she'd admitted to herself that if, by chance, she did meet an incredible man, she wouldn't turn him down. But the way her life had been going, she was not going to hold her breath. Most of the women sent out signals like radio towers, transmitting their intentions to any man who was interested enough to look in their direction. Laura, on the other hand, never returned the interested look of the male population and therefore discouraged most of the possible suitors.

When Jim finally made his move, Laura was not surprised. He made an excuse to talk to her, pretending he was waiting in line to use the piece of equipment she was presently occupying. Apparently, he had scoped out her routine in advance and knew the order of the equipment she would be using.

"Good machine for developing upper abs." She could still hear the first sentence he ever spoke to her, the first time she heard his deep, sensual voice. It sent shivers down her spine. Breathless from nervousness as well as effort, she'd offered little response. "Yeah, I guess so," was all she managed to reply.

Fortunately, Jim was as smooth as he was handsome and as experienced as she was inexperienced. He somehow managed to integrate his routine into hers in such a casual and unobtrusive manner that before she was done with her thirty-minute workout, he already knew her name, age, and place of employment and had arranged a dinner date.

Their six-month courtship proceeded in much the same fashion as their initial meeting had. Jim was the rock-solid, confident leader. Laura

3

followed, succumbed, and fell hopelessly in love with his wisdom, strength, confidence, and unwavering force that directed her life in a new and exciting direction. Jim spoke of her beauty, her naiveté, her Ivory-girl complexion and seemed totally oblivious to her warnings about her unsophisticated upbringing. His motto, which he repeated to her constantly, was, "It's not where you've been that's important, but where you are going." He would always follow that remark with, "Stick with me, babe, and you'll go places you never imagined."

Laura understood she had a lot to learn about living within a new social class. She knew Jim enjoyed the challenge; it was like shaping a raw lump of clay into a beautiful vase. It gave him the opportunity to mold her and shape her to fit into his world. For the first time in her life she felt that she had a purpose in the grand scheme of life, a position to fill, a role to play, and a person she loved dearly to fill the void that had been present for as long as she could remember. Jim provided a solid foundation to build her future upon. It was a life to be proud of, and the best part of it all was her future included this gorgeous, successful man. He once told her that showing her the world and all it had to offer was like seeing it all for the first time, and it helped him appreciate the finer things in life.

Of the time they had spent together thus far, their honeymoon held the fondest memories. The newlyweds chartered a sailboat in the Virgin Islands, a forty-foot sloop. Since Jim had become an accomplished sailor during his college years, he had no difficulties handling the navigation around the islands. The two of them, alone, formed a deep bond that was nurtured and fostered by the elegance of their boat and the beauty of the islands. *It was almost magical*, she thought back wistfully. Suddenly, a flash from a particular moment invaded her more pleasant memories of the trip. Sailing between the Virgin Gorda and Tortola, the day had been perfect. She remembered drinking in the beauty of the crystal-blue water as it rolled along past the bow of their boat, breathing in the scent of the salty sea air, and languishing in the warm rays of tropical sun cooled gently by the ocean breeze. They pulled into a small harbor just in time to see the last rays of the color-injected sunset and spent a happy hour watching the last fragments of color disappear below the horizon. Laura set out their usual happy-hour hors d'oeuvres, and Jim popped open a bottle of savory red wine. As Jim poured the wine into the crystal stemware, he lifted his glass toward the horizon and then toward Laura. He remarked in a mock British accent, "Ah, I wonder what the poor people are doing right now?"

Jim immediately picked up on the look on Laura's face and inquired in a concerned tone, "What's the matter, sweetheart? Did I say something wrong?"

Laura slid over and hugged Jim tightly. She kissed him on the cheek. "You just have no idea, do you?"

"Idea about what? What are you so perplexed about?" he responded.

"What it's like to live on the other side. I do. And all I can say is thank you. Thank you for taking me away from all that pain and emptiness," Laura explained.

Jim looked into her sparkling green eyes and ran his fingers though her long, soft brown hair that gently blew across her face in the gentle evening breeze.

"You never deserved to live that way, Laura. It was all a mistake. You should have been born into a royal family and fed from a silver spoon," he crooned to her playfully.

"I don't know about that …"

Jim pressed his fingers against her lips, once again holding her back from unleashing her memories of the past.

"Stick with me, babe, and you'll forget all about your past."

Laura went to the changing room at the gym and put her duffle bag in her locker. The room was empty this morning, except for her. She stood in front of the large mirror and studied her reflection. She made a vow to herself. The sense of her inadequacies, guilt from finally achieving the fairy-tale life, and doubt that she could live up to the task presented to her of being the model wife were dispelled. As she looked in the mirror, she adjusted her ponytail; she met the gaze of the woman staring back at her and said, "Positive thinking, love for Jim, and hope."

Energized and excited, Laura headed into the gym for her morning workout. It was the first item on the agenda of any model corporate wife.

# Chapter 2

LAURA'S DAILY SCHEDULE HAD PRETTY much been established by her husband since the day they returned from their honeymoon. Jim had insisted that she quit her job as a secretary for "that going nowhere" accounting business and take her time deciding what career she would like to pursue. He hadn't objected to the idea of her working; it was just that he wanted her to be in a position that offered advancement. He wanted her to work for a company that was reputable and that would treat her right. In the meantime, Jim insisted that she start her mornings with a good workout at the club. From there, her day progressed the same way every day of the week. She returned from the club in time to shower again, tidy up the townhouse, and run any small errands she or Jim needed doing. Then she met Jim for lunch precisely at noon. Jim insisted on this quality time together, since he was required many days to stay late at work, and he left for work by 5:00 a.m. each morning. If they missed having dinner together, at least they had spent time together at lunch. Many days, Jim had put in seven hours of nonstop work by noon.

The sleek black BMW rolled easily into the visitor parking space outside Jim's office building. Giving her this car as a gift was just another reminder that Jim did nothing halfway. At work, he was quickly becoming indispensable to the growing marketing research–based company. The company was in the process of expanding into real estate by purchasing large tracts of land and not only researching the development needs of the area but selling the land after it was developed. There was a growing need for retirement homes in their area, as well as higher-priced modern homes for the young executives flooding into the area. Not only were the North Carolina mountains the number-one retirement spot in the country, but industry had seized the fever and began moving their companies into this beautiful, low-cost area as well.

As his boss Tom Sharp would describe him, Jim was a mover and a shaker. Their relationship was one of mutual respect, known rarely in the working world. Tom knew that Jim was an entrepreneur, a person who made things happen. Jim knew that Tom was a planner, a designer, a person with foresight and experience who could see into the future and guide him in the right direction. Not everyone in the company was happy about the relationship between Tom and Jim, and grumbling undercurrents ran through some of the small cliques of employees.

As Laura entered the small but distinct two-story building that Jim's company, Sharp Enterprises, had recently built, she took a deep breath, pulled open the large glass door, and stepped into the lobby. The receptionist recognized Laura immediately from her daily visits to Jim and gave her a pleasant smile. Laura proceeded directly to the elevator. Laura had mentioned to Jim that she might like to work for the company as a receptionist or secretary, but Jim had dismissed the idea, spouting the rule about spouses being employed at the same company.

"Besides," he would tell her, "your best bet is to go to school and get a degree in something you really want to do. For the first time in your life you have the time, money, and opportunity. The sky is the limit for you."

The elevator rode smoothly to the second floor. It was immaculate and still smelled like new carpet. The color palette of the building was deep maroons, black, and beige. Modern art hung on the walls of the hallway and elevator. The door opened automatically, and she stepped into the hallway leading to Jim's new office. Walking down the hallway always made Laura feel like an intruder. Heads would turn from their focus on the important papers they were engrossed with. She always wondered why those people left their doors open if people walking down the hallway were such a distraction. A few of the faces she recognized from Jim's introductions during the few parties she had been to with him. After five years of working for this company, Jim had not developed any personal friendships with his coworkers other than his boss. She reached Jim's office and realized she had been holding her breath as she had walked down the hallway. Chiding herself for still being nervous about meeting her husband at his place of employment, she took a deep breath and paused to knock on

Jim's half-open door. Laura was concealed from Jim's view because his desk was against the far wall. She paused when she heard Jim's familiar voice carrying on a conversation with who could be no one other than Tom.

"I know this particular mountain like the back of my hand. For Christ's sake, I used to camp there when I was in Boy Scouts," she heard Jim say.

"I agree that it is a prime location, Jim," Tom responded, "but you can't build a resort on a mountain you don't own, now can you?"

"There has to be a way for us to obtain that property. Everyone has their price," Jim countered.

"Jim, we offered them more than the current market value for the land, and they declined. There is too much property out there to get upset over one failed deal."

"You're wrong on this one, Tom. The view from this mountain, the picturesque streams, and the gentle slope, ideal for building, would make this place a gold mine. It is just a matter of time before someone talks these hillbillies into selling, and we might as well be the ones that seal that deal."

"Well, I do admit that it is prime property. And the specs on the resort that we would like to build there would be nothing like this area has ever seen. I guess we could brainstorm on a few more ideas for procurement, if you get my meaning. You are right that there probably are ways ... I just don't know," Tom added without conviction.

At that moment, whether by instinct or second nature, Tom peered around the door to find Laura standing there, poised to knock.

"Jim is the luckiest man in the word to have such a beautiful and devoted wife come and meet him for lunch every day." Tom grasped Laura's hand and held it in his own for a moment. He looked her steadily in the eyes and said, "Just make sure you treat him right. He's one of this company's most valuable assets."

Laura withdrew her hand, disturbed by what she had overheard, not letting her emotions surface in front of the two men.

"Believe me; his assets are in good hands."

Tom chuckled and turned toward his office at the end of the hall. She heard the sound of his solid oak door closing as she entered Jim's office. Jim's face lit up immediately, as it always did when she entered the room.

"How is the love of my life? Is it noon already? My, how time flies when you are spending millions."

Laura reached behind her, closed his door, and then walked behind the desk without saying a word. She sat on Jim's lap and looked him in the eyes.

"What mountain were you two talking about when I was standing in the hall?"

"The heart and soul of the Blue Ridge Mountains, Tanner Mountain. Why?"

"Are you really going to build a resort and ruin the beauty of that area?" Laura asked incredulously.

"Now don't go getting all environmentalist on me. We plan on building a noninvasive, environmentally friendly, energy-efficient resort that will allow people to enjoy the beauty of the area, not destroy it. Isn't that why God built this planet, so man could enjoy places like Tanner Mountain?"

"But you said yourself that as a Boy Scout you camped and hiked there. What happens if all the beautiful places are made into resorts? There will be no places left for future Boy Scouts to go camping," Laura argued.

"That is what the parks are for—Grandfather Mountain and all the places the state has reserved for just those purposes."

"I know," Laura conceded. "But don't you remember the feeling you had, being somewhere that wasn't protected by man? Somewhere you could go and wonder if anyone had stepped in the same spot before? Or drink from a stream where the water was so cold and fresh it tasted like it just melted from a glacier?"

"Let's not worry about that now. I'll tell you what. I will personally bring you to the location where we want to build this resort. You can look at the plans and see for yourself how this place will add to the beauty of the mountain, not detract from it, okay?"

"You, my man, have a deal. But I am going to hold you to it. You know, part of protecting an asset such as yourself is helping you to make the right decisions. Besides, it has been months since our honeymoon, and you promised me a weekend of fun and adventure that will rival those two weeks we spent in the islands. It is time you pay up, or I am going to have to find me a husband who lives up to his promises."

"You go ahead and look, sweetheart," Jim responded playfully as he bent Laura over backward and kissed her firmly on the lips, "but just remember you have to give back the Beemer I gave you for a wedding present."

"In that case, I think I will give you a second chance," Laura replied.

"Now, if you'll get off my lap, I can take you out to lunch so I can get back here, finish my work, and get home on time for the first time this week."

Laura slid off Jim's lap, took him by the hand, and led him out of the office. The walk back down the hall didn't bother her in the slightest. When Jim was beside her, people tended to go about their business and not stare at her. Although she could still see furtive glances when the office workers picked their heads up to stare, they quickly looked away when they saw Jim. It was almost as if they feared him. She couldn't understand why the entire world didn't see Jim as she did, a warm, caring, driven, and intelligent man. He'd rescued her from a cold and hostile life and gave her a warmth and love she had never known. Why couldn't these people see this in him? For now, it remained a mystery.

# *Chapter 3*

TWO MORE MONTHS ROLLED BY. Laura still had the impression that she was either in a dream or living someone else's life. She took Jim's advice and enrolled in a few freshman courses at a local community college. She was enrolled in a basic accounting and business course that gave her an introduction to what she could look forward to in the future. She still met Jim for lunch on Tuesdays and Thursdays, and they committed themselves to work out in the gym at least two nights a week so they could share a common activity. Jim was not always able to make the commitment, but Laura was accepting of the fact that sometimes important deals or business meetings had to take precedence over time spent with her.

One night after working out, the couple sat in a quiet booth at a quaint corner bar down the street from the health club. Laura had ordered a white wine spritzer, and Jim ordered his usual brand of imported beer. Since childhood, she could not stand the smell of beer but kept that a secret from Jim because she knew how much he loved his beer. Laura sat staring at his well-chiseled features in the dim lighting and admired the strong lines of his handsome face.

"You know, you need a son," she whispered across the table.

Jim looked up with a start. "I thought we talked about this already. We both agreed that I am working far too much right now to be a devoted father. If I have children, I want to be able to spend time with them, not just see them on weekends."

"I know," Laura said. She glanced down at the table, having expected the response. "It just seems that now is the perfect time for me—biologically, that is—to have a child. I am still in school, so it wouldn't interfere with a career. I am in perfect health and excellent shape. It is a shame that our lives seem to be running on different tracks."

"They are on the same track," Jim implored. "Nothing could be more perfect. We have the ideal life together. You are always there for me when I need you, and you have the freedom to pursue your dreams for once. Having a child would ruin all of that."

"You know, if I didn't know better, Mr. James McBane, I would think you are afraid of change!"

"Me, afraid of change? Ha! I can run rings around you logically. First of all, who is it that doesn't want me to build a resort on her precious mountain? Second of all, I made the biggest change known to man—I married you. I gave up the ultimate bachelor lifestyle, and now I walk around with the proverbial ball and chain."

"Is that what you consider me, a ball and chain?" Laura stated with feigned exacerbation.

"You know that is just a figure of speech," Jim defended. "If you are a ball and chain, then they can shackle me up any day."

"Well, I guess I will accept that as an apology."

"Apology?" Jim leaned across the table and kissed Laura. "When are we going to get into a real fight, anyway? I want to get to the makeup sex," Jim whispered in her ear.

"If you want, we can start one right now." Laura leaned back, changing her tone to a more serious one.

"All right, what's eating you?" Jim asked.

Laura's emotions were bottled up inside of her like shaken soda in a can. She wanted to explode and let all her true feelings come gushing out. She looked down at her hands, her fingers intertwined and her knuckles white from gripping so hard. She was frustrated with her inability to stand up to Jim and discuss her true feelings. She had lost count of the number of times she had broached the baby subject and been shot down by Jim or lost her nerve to push the issue. Now another sore subject was raising its ugly head. Jim was too busy to keep his promise to take her up to see the mountain.

"Two months ago, you promised me that you would personally take me to see the area you are working so vehemently to develop. You said you would let me have an opinion whether this sight would be destroyed or beautified by your resort."

"Yes, I did," Jim confessed. "And I will honor my promise. In fact, let's set a date right now."

Laura straightened up in her seat, surprised by Jim's answer but skeptical. Her eyes lit up, and a whisper of a smile crossed her face.

"Do you mean it?" Laura asked with growing excitement. "You promise this time that nothing will stand in the way of our weekend together—no emergency meetings, unfinished paperwork, breaking deals?"

"I promise. But I do have to be honest with you, Laura." Jim paused, his stare indicating to Laura that what he had to tell her was not going to be good news. "While I do respect your opinion, if we get the green light to go forward on this project, I'm afraid your opinion will not mean a whole lot to the corporations funding this project."

"Wait a minute," Laura interrupted. "I thought that those 'hillbillies,' as you called them, didn't even want to sell the property?"

"How do you know that I referred to those people as hillbillies, and how do you know the status of our offer on the property?" Jim asked, raising his eyebrows and staring sternly at Laura.

"One day when I came to meet you for lunch, I accidentally overheard you and Tom talking," Laura explained.

"You were eavesdropping!"

"No!" Laura defended. "You know me better than that. I just overheard a conversation that sounded important, and I didn't want to interrupt."

"Laura, darling. If you ever come across that situation again, you need to make your presence known. There are certain, shall we say, situations that are not in your best interest to know about."

Stunned, Laura asked, "Are you suggesting that you are into something illegal in your company?"

"No, of course not. I am just saying that in our business, there are certain politics involved. They are not illegal; they are an accepted way of putting pressure on certain people to ensure the future of the company. That is all I am going to say on the matter, except it would be better that as an outsider you were not privy to that sort of information."

"By whose standards are these practices acceptable, Jim?" Laura inquired, her voice beginning to waiver with emotion. "Do you think they are acceptable to the families that have owned property for five generations and are now being strong-armed into selling their family-owned land?"

"Laura," Jim soothed. "Stop and think about what you are saying for a moment. Progress is inevitable. The world is changing. It cannot stay the same way forever. Would you rather have some uncaring, land-hungry developers come in and force these people off their land? At least our company cares about the environment. We will ensure measures are taken to protect the resources that we have. Either we profit from the venture or someone else a lot less ethical than we are does. Surely you can see my point?"

Laura thought for a moment before she answered. "I'm just not sure that picking the lesser of two evils is necessarily the right choice. All my life—"

Jim stopped her before she could finish her observation about her past. "Hey, let's forget about all this right now and plan for our camping trip." Jim pulled out his iPhone and pulled up his daily planner. "It looks like I should be able to get away in three weeks."

Laura started to answer and then closed her mouth and shifted in her seat.

"Three weeks," she said, raising her eyes to meet his. "I was thinking more like a week or two."

"Honestly, if I did plan for a week or two, I would probably end up letting you down again, and I just won't do that. In three weeks this entire proposal should be wrapped up. I will have one weekend to go up to the mountain, and we can take a look and enjoy ourselves. The final meeting and decision is set up for the following Monday. There is nothing more I can possibly do once the proposal is submitted, so you see, it is an ideal time to visit the mountain in all its undisturbed glory."

Once again, Jim's strong sense of guidance and confidence won over Laura's objections.

"All right. Three weeks it is. But it better be a hell of a weekend."

"I promise, babe. Now let's blow this Popsicle stand and head home. It is getting late, and I have to be at work early again tomorrow."

Jim signaled the waitress for the check. Bambi, as her name tag indicated, looked at and spoke directly to Jim. Laura hated it when waitresses acted as if she was invisible and Jim was the only person seated at the table. "Do y'all need anything else, sweetie?" she said as she smiled at Jim.

"No, Bambi, just the check, thank you," he smiled back.

"Yes, we are fine," Laura chimed in. The waitress turned and looked at Laura as if she had just interrupted a private conversation between the two of them. The she directed her attention back to Jim.

"You can either pay me or pay at the register as you leave," Bambi continued. Jim pulled out a twenty and handed it to the waitress, instructing her to keep the change.

Bambi graciously accepted the bill and smiled as if she had just received the biggest tip of the evening. "Why, thank you, sweetheart. Y'all come again," she drawled in her thick southern accent.

"We will," Laura responded, but Bambi had already turned and walked away.

"Don't think I didn't notice the little jealousy bit there with the waitress," Jim pointed out. "She was just being courteous and doing her job."

"Since when is ignoring the woman at the table part of her job?" Laura answered brusquely.

"Honestly, you are so far above that now. You don't need to get defensive because some peon flirted a little to help earn a living," Jim answered.

Laura reflected on that thought for a moment and noticed a pattern in Jim's thinking when it came to his opinion about people not involved in his world. Not responding, she took his hand, and they left the bar. She couldn't decide if she was happy that she was with the upper echelon or more embarrassed than ever that she used to be one of those people that her husband considered peons.

# Chapter 4

THE NEXT MORNING, JIM WAS off to work by 5:00 a.m., as he'd promised. Laura wondered where his energy and drive came from. Lingering feelings from last night's bar episode still clung to her groggy morning thoughts. Once again, the feeling she'd had on the boat, the feeling she'd had in the bar, made her uncertain. Quickly, she reminded herself of the vow she had taken to not look back, only forward. Besides, it was Friday. She was planning on calling Jim when she got home from school to tell him she had a surprise planned for dinner, making sure he would be home at a reasonable hour. While a gourmet cook she was not, she had been educating herself on some of the finer points of cooking. Jim never complained about her cooking but kindly encouraged her to experiment and better her domestic talents. She, in turn, had collected books on cooking, and she watched the Food Network and did her best to duplicate some of the recipes. Her culinary expertise had never been developed in the past because her diet had consisted mainly of peanut butter and jelly, tuna, and Hamburger Helper, sometimes without the hamburger. She did what she could with those ingredients, but their gourmet possibilities were quite limited.

Tonight, she was planning her most extravagant meal ever. She had taken notes on aesthetics when Jim took her out to fine restaurants. She finally had the money to splurge on expensive ingredients. She rushed into the kitchen on the way to her first class to grab a bite to eat and, once again, to check which ingredients she would need to purchase on the way home. Grabbing her knapsack full of books, she rushed out the front door and went out to her shiny car, a constant reminder to her of the change in her lifestyle. Throwing her bag in the backseat, she paused, hearing a woman's voice call her name.

"Laura, you're off in such a hurry this morning!"

It was one of the few neighbors she had met. While she had not struck up any friendships, she and Eileen spoke in a pleasant, neighborly sort of way whenever they happened to meet. A wave of embarrassment swept over Laura. Eileen had been pregnant, expecting, what was it now, a week ago? Laura had been so wrapped up in her own life that she hadn't had the courtesy to find out if Eileen had delivered and to bring her a gift.

"Oh my goodness, Eileen, you had the baby! I am so sorry I didn't stop by and see you," Laura said anxiously.

"Believe me, I haven't been ready for any company anyway. My mom has been staying with me to help out and all, but having a newborn is more work than two people can handle," Eileen confessed.

Laura moved closer to take a look at the delicately wrapped pink bundle in the stroller. "She doesn't bite!" Eileen laughed, sensing Laura's hesitation. "Here," she said, and she stooped down to lift the baby from the carriage. "Meet Ellen Rose."

Hesitantly, Laura took the baby from Eileen, careful to support the tiny head. She did not remember ever having held a baby before; the feeling was foreign and yet not uncomfortable. She pressed the baby gently to her chest and nestled her in the crook of her arm.

"She is so tiny and precious," Laura admired. A single tear rolled its way down Laura's cheek. Laura lifted the baby's head to her cheek and felt the downy softness of the baby's hair. She breathed in the scent of baby powder and the delicate scent that only comes from newborns. She became almost dizzy from the impact this had on her senses.

"God, she is so beautiful. What a precious little angel." Laura carefully handed the baby back to her mother.

"You are so lucky, Eileen," Laura managed to say even though she felt as if her throat had constricted from holding back her tears.

"I know. The instant your baby is born, you develop this bond that is so strong, you can't even believe it is possible. Those little eyes look into yours, and you can just tell that this tiny miracle you carried around for nine months already knows who you are."

Laura watched as the mother carefully tucked the bundle back into the carriage. "I guess you and your husband will be planning a family soon?" Eileen winked as she smiled at Laura.

"Soon, I guess," was all that Laura was able to respond.

"Well, let me tell you from firsthand experience. There is nothing greater in all the world than having your first child. It makes the entire world seem right, and it brings you and your husband together in a way that nothing else could. Together you created a miracle, and the love you share for that child is like nothing else you'll ever experience in this lifetime."

Laura cleared her throat. "I'm really happy for you, Eileen, and I promise I'll stop by this weekend and bring by the gift I bought for you two." Laura lied about having a gift, but she didn't want this woman to think she was so preoccupied with her own life that she didn't have time to think about others.

"You didn't have to get me anything," Eileen replied courteously. "But feel free to stop by with your husband to give him a preview of what he is missing."

"I will," Laura answered, hoping that if she did, the baby would have the same effect on Jim that it did on her.

Laura hurried through the rest of her day and returned with the necessary ingredients to prepare her gourmet meal. She'd had trouble concentrating during her classes. Seeing her neighbor's baby had an effect on her that she just couldn't shake. Perhaps this evening, after a romantic candlelight dinner, she would once again approach her husband about having a baby. After all, how could he deny her maternal instincts simply because it wasn't the right time for him? *Damn it*, it was the right time for her. This was important to her. He had to have a better reason than his work schedule for not fulfilling this part of their lives. She had never really stood up to Jim on any point before. This was going to be the first test of how much leverage she actually had in the marriage. She had no experience standing up to any men in her life, and the mere thought of it gave her butterflies and caused her face to flush.

After putting away the groceries, Laura picked up the phone but paused before dialing her husband's number. She struggled with what she should say to him. Should she tell him that she had something important to discuss or just spring it on him at the right time? She closed her eyes and prayed for guidance in the decision. Although not deeply religious, Laura had a personal relationship with God that developed from the need to have some source of strength in her life when all the people around her failed in that department. All the difficult times she lived through, sometimes praying was the only thing that made her feel better. She waited for some sort of divine signal but didn't receive any. She knew she was alone on this one.

Jim's secretary patched her through, and the sound of Jim's voice on the phone almost caused her to hang up. "Jim! Hello, sweetie, it's just me."

"Laura, I'm not used to you calling this time of day. Is everything okay?"

"Of course. I just called you to let you in on a little surprise. I'm in the process of creating a culinary masterpiece, and you are the guest of honor at tonight's feast, so don't be late!" she demanded.

Jim paused and then asked, "Did you find out about my surprise? Is that why I am getting the royal treatment?"

"Your surprise? What are you talking about, Jim?"

"Never mind," he teased. "I might be a few minutes late tonight, but I promise it will be worth the wait."

"Jim, this is not fair. It was supposed to be my evening for surprises. How could you do this to me?"

"Well, if you don't want it, just let me know, and I'll be home on time for dinner."

"You know darn well that I want … whatever it is. But I went to a lot of work for this meal, and you better not spoil it by being too late. Remember, there is nothing more dangerous than a woman scorned."

"Or a dinner scorched. I've had your cooking, remember?" Jim added sarcastically.

"You are evil, Jim McBane. You are going to eat those words, literally. All right, I love you. I will see you tonight." Laura hung up the phone with a hundred unanswered questions still lingering in her mind.


Laura spent the next few hours torn between trying to concentrate on preparing the meal, wondering what surprise her husband had in store for her, and deciding how to bring up the subject of wanting to have a baby. She had to remake the white sauce three times because she kept losing her concentration and scorching the ingredients. Finally, dinner was prepared and the finishing touches completed. Laura wiped the counter for the third time, making sure the surface was spotless. She peeked in the oven at the loaf of warming bread and turned each spice bottle in the spice rack so the labels were facing the same direction. The table was covered with a white lace tablecloth she had just purchased, and the table was set with the fine china they had received from Jim's aunt for their wedding. It had only been used a few times during their marriage because Laura never felt her meals were worthy of their elegance. Jim was always too busy and wanted to spend his spare time alone with Laura, so they never had company over. None of Jim's family had visited since their wedding, and Laura had lost all touch with her family members.

The silver candlesticks sat on each side of the fresh flower arrangement she had picked up from the florist on her way home from school. The long-stemmed wineglasses added an elegant accompaniment to the array of silverware beside each plate. Laura had made sure that each piece was arranged properly because Jim would comment if something was out of place. She had Googled how to set a formal table and wanted everything about this evening to be perfect.

She heard the soft rumble of Jim's Mercedes enter the driveway and the sound of the automatic garage doors sliding open. The engine cut off, and Laura was nervous with anticipation and excitement. She took off her apron and gave herself a quick glance in the mirror. She had put on a simple yet sexy black cocktail dress and styled her hair to fall down over her shoulders in a way she knew her husband loved. She wiped a spot of flour off her cheek and smiled at how clichéd this whole scenario appeared: the doting housewife cooking the perfect meal for her hardworking husband. It could have been a scene out of *Desperate Housewives*.

Smiling at her last thought, she heard Jim shouting from the garage. "Laura, I want you to sit down in the kitchen and close your eyes."

What kind of a surprise is this?" Laura wondered out loud. All her efforts to make the evening perfect were lost. Whatever Jim's surprise was, it was upstaging her dinner plans. Once again, she felt a responsibility to do what Jim asked and play the part of the obedient housewife. She felt let down and disappointed.

"Are you ready?" Jim shouted.

"I'm ready!" Laura shouted back, wondering what the neighbors were thinking about all the yelling going on.

Laura heard the door open and the sound of Jim's footsteps enter the kitchen. She listened for a clue as to what his surprise might be, because at this point she had no idea. Jim stepped closer and she could feel him next to her face. *Did he get a new haircut?* She didn't think so. *Maybe he's wearing a tuxedo and has two tickets for the opera.* Suddenly, Jim's face pressed so close to hers that she felt his warm breath against her cheek. She kept her eyes glued shut. Then he licked her. Laura couldn't stand it any longer; her eyes popped open. Staring at her were a big pair of soft, brown puppy eyes.

"A puppy?" Laura exclaimed.

"I thought you needed some company during the day, and this little guy volunteered," explained Jim.

"Is this a Golden Retriever?" Laura asked inquisitively.

"It is. Best bloodlines, pick of the litter."

Laura was speechless. A tumult of emotions coursed through her brain at that moment.

"Well?" insisted Jim. "Isn't he gorgeous? I decided we should name him Alex after my favorite adventure hero, Alex Cross. I hope he will be as smart and cunning." He handed the puppy over to his stunned wife.

"Yes, he is beautiful. But this is so unlike you. I never even knew you liked animals," Laura admitted.

"Dogs are okay, as long as they are kept clean and are housebroken. I was thinking of you when I got him, your needs. I've seen your look of disappointment whenever we talk about waiting to have a baby. I was hoping this would ease the waiting period."

Laura couldn't make up her mind whether to laugh or cry. The whole evening's plan was shattered. Laura knew that his use of the term "waiting period" meant that the topic was officially off limits and that Jim had no intention of letting her get pregnant. She knew that he had made a concession by bringing home a pet, and this was as close to having a baby as he would let her get. She had mentioned getting a cat when they were engaged, and Jim made it quite clear that no pets would be allowed in his new townhouse, ever. She had never even brought up the subject again.

"He is adorable. Thank you, sweetheart," Laura said without much enthusiasm. She couldn't help her look of disappointment.

"You don't look very happy. I thought you loved animals, especially dogs," Jim stated with concern.

"I do. I love animals. I guess it is just so out of character for you to buy me this that I am still in shock."

Jim took the puppy off her lap and placed it gently on the floor. Then he pulled Laura to her feet. He wrapped his strong arms around her neck and burrowed his head in her soft, fragrant hair. He kissed her gently on the top of her forehead.

"I love you, Laura. You look beautiful tonight, by the way. I am starved. Let's eat," he said, without a single comment about the gorgeous table Laura had so carefully prepared.

The puppy sat at their feet, staring up at the two of them, as if waiting for instructions on what to do next. When he didn't get any reaction from his new owners, he barked in his sharp puppy voice. Laura and Jim looked down and laughed at the expression of concern on the puppy's face. Laura squatted down and took the puppy's head in her hands. She noticed for the first time the soft texture of his golden fur and the intelligence portrayed in his bright little eyes.

"I can see already that you are going to be a demanding little man," she said softly to Alex.

The three of them ate Laura's gourmet meal by soft candlelight, the soothing tones of jazz music playing in the background. No answers were given to Laura that evening on the topic of when she would be allowed to have a baby. The discussion never even came up. But in some small way, Alex filled the need she had to care for someone. While she loved her husband deeply, there was very little room to provide the nurturing she felt she needed to give to another being. Alex responded immediately to her warm embraces and whined and cried whenever she put him down or stopped paying attention to him.

The two new parents went to bed, intending that Alex would sleep in his crate in the corner of the kitchen. But after an hour of whimpering, neither one of them could stand to hear the puppy cry any longer, so the crate was moved into their room. Not long after that move, the puppy was fast asleep between Laura and Jim. Laura dreamed that night of puppies and babies. In her dream, people kept staring at her because she was carrying a puppy dressed like a baby. When a woman in her dream asked her why she was pushing a puppy around in the stroller, she told the woman that this was her baby. Laura did not remember the dream when she woke up the next morning.

# *Chapter 5*

THE WEEKEND PASSED. LAURA AND Jim were preoccupied with establishing a routine to housebreak the new family member. Jim refused to visit Eileen and the new baby. He made one excuse after another, so Laura waited until Monday while Jim was at work to deliver the gift she had purchased over the weekend. Once again, she held the newborn and felt the stirring of motherhood deep in her soul. But when she returned to her home and felt the joy the puppy exuded at seeing her return, she dispelled the thoughts about bringing up the baby issue. She thought to herself that maybe it would be okay to wait a little longer. The puppy would certainly be a handful for the next year or so.

The next three weeks flew by. Between school and the puppy, every moment of Laura's time was occupied. She never dreamed puppies could be so much work. Her morning ritual changed immediately, because she had to wake up early and take the puppy out, first thing. There were no more leisurely mornings of sleeping in and taking a shower and heading off to start the day at her own pace. Jim insisted that she take responsibility for the puppy because he did not have time to fool with it before work. Since the puppy was only partially housetrained, Laura had to maintain a strict schedule, taking the puppy out for a walk every two hours. She couldn't bear to think of the disastrous consequences of having the puppy stain one of Jim's new carpets. She also had to occupy the puppy by constantly playing with it. If left to amuse himself, Alex would find inappropriate objects to chew on to appease his voracious appetite to play.

The Friday finally arrived for Jim and Laura's camping outing to Tanner Mountain. Jim kept his promise; he bought some camping equipment after work one evening. Laura was excited that her puppy would experience the thrill of being in the wilderness. His only knowledge of the outside world so far consisted of cement sidewalks and sparse lawns. He had only been to a park a few times and had never been allowed off the leash. When Laura thought about her own recent change in lifestyle, she realized that she had missed the mountains. She closed her eyes and remembered the familiar scents and sounds of the forest. *I miss those mountains—the smell of the air mixed with the scent of pine, the rustling sounds of chipmunks and squirrels as they dash from tree to tree, and long solitary walks in the woods. I can remember pretending the giant trees were my guardians, standing watch over me, their gigantic limbs protective arms hovering over me. I remember spending the night in the woods with nothing but a blanket and feeling ten times safer than being in the house with my father.*

As a child, she had spent hours exploring every facet of the mountains, often sleeping alone rather than face the horrors at home. She was never frightened of being alone because she figured there was no fate worse than being trapped in the house with her father during one of his drunken rampages. She put the memories behind her and concentrated on packing the food and supplies they would need for their camping weekend.

Jim came home too late from work to depart on their trip Friday night, but he promised they would leave first thing in the morning. Laura had missed her Friday courses at school just to make sure that everything was prepared for the trip. She was disappointed, once again, that they wouldn't be leaving as scheduled, but she was consoled by the fact that at least the trip wasn't canceled.

Morning arrived, and the trio packed into Laura's BMW. Jim charted their course on his GPS. Methodical as usual, Jim left nothing to chance, and Laura knew that even though Jim had not been to the mountain in years, they would reach their destination without event. He even brought a map in case there was no reception in the mountains, and he circled the spot on the map where they would park the car and hike to their camping spot. They would end up on the side of the mountain where the proposed building site would be located. There were several spots in the area to set up their tent and make a campsite.

When they were out of the town and began the ascent up the mountain roads, Laura's excitement mounted. Maybe it wouldn't be such a bad thing if the resort was built. Perhaps she and Jim and Alex could even live there. The puppy sat in her lap and panted tensely, trying to watch each object as it passed quickly past the window. He finally got dizzy and lay his head down in Laura's lap. Jim and Laura rode in silence, each occupied with their own set of thoughts.

As the elevation of the road increased, the views became breathtaking. Laura struggled with her emotions, realizing she had totally forgotten the beauty and majesty of the mountains. The road climbed upward, and she peered out over the ever-deepening valleys. The full view of the seemingly unending forest of trees spread below them. In the distance, tiny houses appeared, insignificant within the grandeur of nature surrounding them. Gigantic boulders perched precariously along the road, hints of the powerful rockslides that occasionally took place. Now and again, a stream would appear as if out of nowhere and flow back into the ground, disappearing into the vastness of the vegetation. During the drive, Laura became totally lost in her observations of the spectacular scenery around her. Jim must have sensed this or been lost in his own thoughts, because they did not speak until they reached the dirt road that would deposit them at the base of their hike.

"Here we are. Hold on, because the ride may get a bit bumpy. There is no telling what shape this road is in," Jim announced.

Laura awoke from her trance and noticed the puppy was still sound asleep in her lap. She couldn't believe how much Alex had grown in just three weeks. He was almost too big to sit in her lap comfortably, but she didn't have the heart to break the news to him.

"I can't believe we are here already." Laura's excitement woke the puppy, and he sprang up and resumed his watch out the window. The car was moving more slowly on the dirt road than the main road, and the puppy could follow the objects with interest. Laura rolled down the window partway so Alex could stick his nose out and catch the scents of the forest.

"It is a good thing we both keep in good shape," Jim noted. "Otherwise, we might be biting off a bit more than we could chew."

Laura reminded him, "This is where I grew up, Jim, and there is nothing about these mountains that I can't handle."

"Okay, Jane—me Tarzan. You and your little chimp over there better not fall behind, because we don't slow down for nobody," Jim teased.

"Oh, yeah?" Laura couldn't help but retort. "I'll wager I can climb circles around you, city boy. Just because you spent a year or two in Boy Scouts does not make you Daniel Boone."

"You're on. How about we have a little race to the top?" Jim taunted.

Naturally competitive, Laura thought about taking him up on the offer. However, she realized that racing up the mountain would take away from the enjoyable quality time, which was the main reason they were there. There was also Alex to think about. Whoever towed him along would have a distinct disadvantage.

"Why don't we take our time and have a leisurely stroll to the campsite? That way, we can enjoy the sights instead of trying to kill ourselves," Laura suggested.

"Chicken, aren't you?"

"Oh, shut up, Jim. You just can't stand it when I have a better idea than you."

Jim paused at her statement and started to tense up. Then he laughed and under his breath said, "That will be the day."

Laura heard the comment but chose to let it go.


The dirt road narrowed and came to an end. A small area provided parking places for a few vehicles, but no others were present on this particular weekend.

"A gorgeous May weekend and not another soul in sight. This is my idea of a perfect weekend," Jim said with growing excitement.

"Yeah, and let's remember that in a few months, if your proposal goes through, this area will be riddled with roads and people, and no one else will be allowed to experience this serenity," Laura pointed out.

"I told you to stop thinking of it on those terms. There are plenty of other uninhabited places for people to camp, and we are providing the opportunity for many people to enjoy this mountain," Jim defended.

Laura looked over at Jim. "You don't have to pitch the sale to me, remember? My opinion doesn't count anyway. I know the reality of the situation is based on whose pocket the profit goes into, not the best interest of nature lovers."

Jim opened the car door, choosing not to respond to Laura's comment. Alex took the opportunity to escape the confines of the car and bolted out before Laura or Jim could grab him.

"Alex!" Jim yelled after the exuberant canine. Alex paused and lifted his nose in the air. He sniffed, his whole body quivering with the excitement of the smells drifting to him from the forest. Jim made his move and grabbed the dog, quickly attaching the leash that Laura had handed to him.

"I guess we better keep him on the leash," Jim warned, noticing how engrossed the dog was in his new surroundings. Laura knelt down beside Alex and took his head in her hands, as she was accustomed to doing whenever she had something serious to discuss with him.

"Alex, if you want to get off this leash and explore, you need to remember to come when we call you."

Jim smiled. "Do you honestly think that dog can understand what you are saying to him? I guarantee he would bolt and never look back if given the opportunity."

"He does understand the tone of my voice and that this is a serious matter. I believe that animals understand more than we think. They just can't communicate back to us. They definitely pick up on the mood of their owners," Laura replied.

Alex's attention turned from the forest. He stepped on Laura's lap and tried to lick her face. He seemed to acknowledge her comment.

"See, Jim, he understands I was trying to explain something to him, even though he might not know exactly what it was."

"No comment," Jim said as he handed the leash to Laura and turned to begin unpacking their supplies from the car. "You two come on over here and get your share of the load to carry. No exceptions for women and dogs on this camping trip."

"Oh, do you plan on strapping saddlebags to the dog and using him as a pack mule?" Laura inquired.

"If need be. I'll wait and see how much I can pack you with first."

"Pack this!" Laura yelled, and she dove and pulled Jim down to the ground and wrestled him underneath her. She was quite strong for a woman of her size, and Jim could feel her strength as he pretended to struggle to overturn her. He was in decent shape also and could have easily turned the struggle in his favor. Instead he said, "Uncle," and admitted defeat.

"All right, I won't make the dog carry the tent, and I'll go easy on your pack. Satisfied?"

"That's more like it," Laura said triumphantly. At that moment, Alex bounded over and jumped into the melee. He headed straight for Jim's face and licked him while Jim warded off his wet, slobbering dog kisses.

Laura laughed and let go of Jim's arms so the puppy wouldn't accidentally scratch Jim's face in his exuberance.

Half an hour later, Jim helped Laura into her pack and eased his own on from the trunk of the car.

"I guess the car will be safe here," Jim said without conviction.

"It will be fine," Laura assured. "We will be back tomorrow night. Besides, the kind of people who come up here are not usually robbers."

"I'm just afraid of vandalism. Monday's meeting is life or death for me, and I am depending on this vehicle to return me to civilization by Sunday evening."

"You will get home for your meeting. If something happened to the car, you'd fashion a hang glider out of the tent and fly home, I have no doubt," Laura joked.

Jim led the way, and Laura and Alex took up the rear. The group followed a barely visible trail that wound its way upward into the dense forest. Jim held a map and a compass in front of him, relying on the orienteering skills he had been taught in Boy Scouts.

"How in the world did you corporate geeks ever pick this location to build a resort?" came Laura's voice from behind him. "I can't imagine any of the individuals funding this project have made this hike themselves."

"Helicopters. They fly over in helicopters and determine which locations would be suitable for development. Actually, we have had a group of surveyors up here already. We should see some red flags tied to trees to indicate the boundaries of the tract of land we will be purchasing. "

The group continued in relative silence, except for Laura's gentle commands for Alex to stay with her and keep up. It was exhilarating for her to see the world through Alex's eyes and watch him experience nature for the first time. He would often tug at the leash, trying to sniff an area where he smelled an animal had been. Sometimes he would determine that he would rather be going in a different direction and bolt quickly in hopes that his efforts would lead to his freedom. Laura knew that Jim was right that if Alex did get off his leash, he would disappear in an instant.

They traveled with relative ease and made a good five miles in half a day, even though the hike was uphill most of the way. Lunchtime arrived. The hikers came to an outcropping of rock that protruded beyond the trees and allowed them a spectacular platform for their picnicking pleasure. They unpacked the sandwiches and ate their lunch, looking out over the spectacular view. Alex forgot his new lust for nature and sat at their feet, eyeing every bite of food that passed their lips. His patience was rewarded at the end of lunch when he was allowed a crust from Laura and half of Jim's second ham and cheese sandwich. Laura and Jim just sat for a while, dangling their feet over the edge of the precipice, neither one bothered by the drop straight down in front of them.

"Nothing but forest and valley as far as the eye can see," Jim noted. "You can't tell me you wouldn't enjoy waking up in the morning and having this for your view."

"Honestly, I did think about how nice it would be to live up here again, "Laura replied. "You forget that this used to be my home."

Jim got to his feet and stretched a moment before putting his pack back on. He took a deep breath of the fresh mountain air and walked to the edge of the precipice. The outcropping consisted of large boulders piled upon one another. The stone Jim was standing on was a large, flat piece of shale. Bits and shards had eroded and fallen away over the years, leaving interesting shapes protruding from the edges. As Jim was noticing these shapes, his eyes followed the trail downward to where smaller rocks and boulders had become dislodged, creating a stationary river of smaller stones.

"Jim, don't get too close to the edge. If you fall, not only would it be a long time before help arrived, but you might be late for your Monday morning meeting."

Jim turned back from the edge. All ears perked toward a rustling in the branches along the treelined side of the outcropping. Alex, in his excitement, bolted to investigate. He pulled away from Laura's relaxed grip on the end of the leash. As he flew by, Jim jumped forward quickly to step on the end of the leash and prevent him from escaping. His leading hiking boot never reached the end of the leash because under his back foot, loose shale splintered, causing him to lose his balance and fall backward.

In one sickening second, Laura reached out to grab Jim's arm as he pinwheeled for balance, only to see him disappear over the edge of the cliff. Time seemed to stand still, and for one brief second, millions of thoughts coursed through Laura's mind as she heard Jim's shout and saw him flailing and finally disappearing over the edge of the cliff. One part of her wanted to turn and flee as fast as she could to try to find help for her husband. The other part of her wanted to rush over to the edge and peer over to see if by some miracle he was clinging just below the outcropping. In the back of her mind, she knew her puppy was probably running away after some small quarry, running farther and farther way from possible recovery.

*Think, for God's sake, think, Laura.* She usually prided herself on staying calm in tense situations, but at the moment all she could do was stand, frozen, full of fear.

*"Jim,"* she shouted hesitantly. *"Jim, can you hear me?"*

Fearful that the shale would break under her weight, she crept to the edge and lay down flat on her stomach. Slowly and carefully she inched her way forward until her torso was hanging over the edge of the precipice so she could view the scene below her.

Directly below her, a large boulder was lodged beneath the overhanging precipice. Suddenly, a hand appeared and then another. Jim emerged, pulling his way up the outside of the boulder. Laura screamed his name again, and the dazed but otherwise uninjured Jim responded breathlessly.

"I'm all right, Laura. When I pull myself to the top of the boulder, grab the back of my pack and help pull me up."

Laura was thankful that she was strong and in good shape. Confidently, she gripped Jim's pack and helped hoist him back up on the ledge.

As soon as he was safely up, Laura threw her arms around him and sobbed into his shoulder.

"I thought you were dead," she cried. "Why didn't you answer when I called to you?"

"Frankly, I didn't hear you. I was worried if I called to you I might lose my grip and fall hundreds of feet to my death."

"What happened? How did you manage to keep yourself from falling all the way down the cliff?" Laura managed to ask.

"When I rolled over the edge, I slid down the big boulder, and I thought I was a goner. Fortunately, there was an indent in the big boulder beneath the ledge, and I was able to stop myself from sliding any farther down. From there I was able to hold on with just brute strength and pull myself back up the rock," Jim narrated, still breathing heavy, his body pumping with adrenaline. Jim stroked Laura's hair and rubbed her back. "I promise, babe, I won't fall over any more cliffs, as long as that dog ... where is the dog?"

Laura looked up from Jim's shoulder in the direction Alex had first run. *"Alex,"* she shouted. But she heard not the faintest rustle of underbrush.

The woods were unnaturally quiet. She put her head back down on Jim's shoulder and began crying again.

"I don't know if I can handle this, Jim," she sobbed.

"Don't worry. Remember the talk you had with him? We'll find him or he'll find us. He loves you, and somehow you two will find each other again. I promise."

Jim pulled Laura away from him and dried her tears with his sleeve. He guided her from the edge of the rocks and put their packs together a safe distance from the edge. Laura could tell he was shaken and that he needed a moment to regroup. He hated not being in control of every situation. "Let's make camp here. We'll stay close and search the area. My bet is that he is warm and safe in your sleeping bag by nightfall," Jim assured Laura.

# Chapter 6

In about an hour, Jim set up the tent a safe distance from the outcropping while Laura searched the woods in the immediate vicinity. She repeatedly called Alex's name and searched for any signs that the dog had been in the area—footprints, broken branches, or even a small animal that he might have killed. Finding not even a shred of evidence, Laura sat down and waited for Jim to finish setting up the tent. She sat on a rock with her knees to her chest; her arms wrapped tightly around her legs and held back the impulse to start rocking. She couldn't shake her sense of foreboding.

"I don't think Alex has enough sense about the outdoors to find his way back here," Laura stated sadly.

Jim stopped pounding in tent stakes a moment and put his arms around her. "Look, we will spend from now till dark looking for him. If we don't find him tonight, we can spend all day tomorrow searching. I know these are big woods and you feel as if you are looking for a needle in a haystack, but you have to remember one thing. Alex loves you as much as you love him. Come suppertime, he is going to be trying to find you."

Laura managed a smile, "I guess you are right. I'll try to stay positive."

"Now that's my girl. I'm almost done setting up the tent. Then I will get my compass and map so we don't get ourselves lost, and we'll set off in the direction we last saw him go."

Jim finished pounding in the tent stakes and then disappeared into the tent, where he had carefully placed all their supplies. He reappeared with a map and compass. He'd strapped a water bottle and flashlight to his belt.

Laura let Jim lead her into the woods and pick the path of least resistance through the thick foliage. Laura suspected that her tracking abilities were better than Jim's, but she let Jim outline his ideas. His plan was to walk a hundred yards, call the dog's name, look for signs, then walk another hundred yards, and repeat the process until they'd covered a few miles. He then wanted to proceed up the mountain at ninety degrees to the direction they had come, and triangulate until they arrived back at their campsite. If Alex wasn't found, they would continue this type of search in a different direction first thing in the morning.

Jim did most of the looking for signs and Laura did most of the calling, since the puppy was more familiar with her voice. After two hours of searching, Laura's voice began to get hoarse. Both of them were tired, not only from the rigorous day's climb but from the emotional turmoil they had endured.

Darkness began to descend like a black veil, covering the mountaintops. A colorful sunset nestled into the valley below them. If the circumstances had been different, they would have been in awe of its brilliance. But weary and discouraged, they completed the last leg of the triangle back to the tent without the slightest sign of Alex.

Back at the tent, the final curtain of darkness having descended fully upon the mountainside, Jim struggled with the small pile of kindling he had collected before their search. "I guess it's been a while since I last started a campfire," he observed as he blew on the dying embers that only moments before had been burning brightly.

"You need to put some larger sticks on top of the smaller ones so the flames can take hold of something and not die out," Laura instructed.

Jim glanced back. "I know what I am doing. I used to be a Boy Scout, remember?"

"Well, obviously you've forgotten your skills during your years of using self-lighting logs in your fireplace."

"Look, if you think you can do a better job, go ahead. Be my guest," Jim said with mild irritation.

Laura confidently moved toward the small embers and in a matter of a few minutes had a small but strong blaze started. She could sense Jim's discomfort with the fact that she had the better survival skills. She didn't bother explaining that starting fires with only the bare essentials had been an integral part of her childhood. She had tried on several occasions to share with Jim some of the details about her childhood, but he changed the subject every time. He was like a brick wall when it came to listening to her about her past.

The two sat around the growing fire in silence. The woods around them echoed with the same eerie silence. The blackness was so complete outside the circle of flames that Laura could not even make out the silhouettes of the trees. A blanket of clouds had moved in shortly after sunset and effectively cushioned even the slightest shimmer of starlight or moonlight from reaching the mountain. The occasional crackle of firewood was the only sound—not a whisper of air from the magnitude of forest that surrounded them, not a single chirp from any of the millions of insects that inhabited the forest.

Laura shivered and wrapped her blanket tightly around her. They had hoped that the puppy would be drawn to the light and the fire, but as the evening waned, so did their hopes. For the first time in their blissful marriage, Laura realized that she may have been confusing some of her feelings. Could she be confusing love with security? Right now, she did not feel close to her husband. She began to realize how superficial their relationship really was. It was built on a paper foundation. There was nothing substantial on which their relationship was built because it was all one-sided, based on Jim's vision of the future. It seemed to her that, taken out of his element, there was less to Jim than she had first imagined. His impetus in life was to move forward, climb that ladder of success. He was wonderful at envisioning and being a driving force in making his visions reality. That is why he was so successful at work. But remove him from the climb and what was left? It was almost as if standing still, even for a moment, was painful for him. He knew relatively nothing of her past and seemed to have an aversion to learning more about it. He loved what she could be, her potential. If he couldn't love who she once was, she wondered if that was like loving half a person. Sometimes the past is almost as important as the future, she reflected, because good or bad, it developed a person's character. It provided a doorway into understanding emotions and reactions to certain situations, and Laura was sure Jim did not understand how upset she really was about losing her puppy.

Settling into mutual gloom, they both decided to crawl into their sleeping bags and renew their search in the morning. Laura kissed her husband good-night and accepted his attempts to apologize for the unfairness of the situation. Within minutes, Laura heard the change in

Jim's breathing that indicated he was asleep. She couldn't expect him to feel the same sense of loss and grief that she felt. She tried to convince herself that with the new day would come renewed hope of finding Alex. Somehow, her heart couldn't accept what her mind was telling her, and positive thinking was not a sufficient barrier to quell the wave of doubts. Laura buried her face in the small camping pillow and cried. She cried for the injustice of not being able to share the pain of her past with her husband and having to suffer with the memories in silence. She cried for Alex being alone, cold, and frightened in a new and hostile environment. She ached to hold him and stroke his soft fur and feel the warmth that his body radiated. She cried for what might have been, if this trip had gone the way it had been planned. The three of them should have been together, happy, enjoying the mountain, stretching the limits of mind and body away from the confines of the daily routines and stresses of their normal lives. Most of all, she cried because she knew she was kidding herself. She and Jim were two very different people striving to fit together like two irregular puzzle pieces. At first appearance they seemed to fit, but when closely examined, the colors didn't quite match up, and the differences in their shapes became more obvious. And lastly she cried for the emptiness left inside her, knowing that her dreams of becoming a mother and having a baby of her own to hold and love were slipping through her fingers.

Finally, somewhere in the semiconscious stage between awareness and sleep, Laura imagined a perfect life. She saw herself sitting on a blanket in a meadow, the mountains visible in the background. On the blanket was a figure she couldn't make out, but the sense of love emanating from him portrayed him as her significant other. Her Golden Retriever bounded through the field around them, searching for tantalizing smells in each new crevice he explored. And on the blanket, between her and the man, lay a baby. She reached her hand toward the baby and stroked its tiny face. The baby reached up and grabbed a finger, its tiny hand just big enough to get a grip around her index finger. Blackness flooded in and removed the scene, and Laura drifted into a dreamless and restless slumber.

Sunlight filtered slowly over the peak of the mountain; its spreading rays shone like silvery beams down into the valley below. Laura woke to hear Jim rustling outside the tent. He had difficulty shutting off his internal alarm system on weekends, when he didn't have to be awake early. Laura's first impressions were of the dampness of her clothing and sleeping bag from the morning dew and the aroma of crisp mountain air mingled with the scent of ashes from last night's fire. Jim was obviously trying to redeem his reputation as master of his domain by trying to relight the fire before Laura woke up. Despite the sick feeling that still lingered over the loss of her puppy, she had to smile at Jim's almost childlike persistence that he had to be the most competent of the two when it came to camping.

Laura sat up and ran her tongue over her teeth, feeling the layer of plaque that mysteriously developed while she slept. She ran her fingers through her hair and pulled some dry clothes out of her backpack. She quickly changed and exited the tent to find that Jim had succeeded in restarting the fire. He had water in a pan and was attempting to boil the water so that they might have their morning coffee.

"Good morning, sunshine," Jim said as she emerged from the tent, the tone of his voice sounding slightly bitter to Laura.

"I see you got the fire started. No sign of Alex, I presume?"

"Yes, I got the fire started, no problem, and no, no signs of Alex. We will have some breakfast, pack up everything, and then start our search again. We can only give it a few hours, and then I want to head back to the car."

Laura suddenly had an idea. "Why don't you leave me here? I will look for Alex, and you can come back and get me in a few days. I am bound to find him by then."

"Don't be ridiculous. I'm not going to leave you up here by yourself. Plus, you don't have enough food to last you past this weekend."

"It was just a thought," Laura explained, dejected by how quickly he shot down her idea.

"Help me start packing up while the water is heating," Jim ordered.

They broke the tent down and packed it away quickly, and all but the food and pots were packed back into their bundles. Laura had no appetite for breakfast but managed to drink a cup of coffee.

When the dishes and pans were rinsed with their minimal supply of water, they packed the last items. Jim pulled out the map to see which direction he thought they should cover. The area where the dog first disappeared had been covered yesterday, and the area back toward the car would be covered on the return hike, so Jim decided to climb down the mountain, rationalizing that maybe the dog was trying to find its way home.

Their last attempt at rescue took the couple down the steep grade of the mountain. They picked the gentlest slope to traverse down and repeated the process of sign-searching and calling Alex's name. They reached the bottom of the mountain in an hour, walked around the woods at its base, and then decided to start the hike back up. Each passing hour made their attempt seem more futile. They also knew that traveling back up the mountain would be much more difficult than the climb down had been, and they would still face a several-hour hike back to the car.

After they climbed back to the campsite, Jim and Laura slumped down in exhaustion. While both of them enjoyed above-average fitness, they were not used to the aerobic conditioning it took to climb a mountain. Laura seemed in a bit better shape than Jim, although she did not point this out to him. Once again, they sat in silence, both regretting that they were going to have to leave shortly, dashing any hopes that they were going to return with the puppy. They sat side by side, taking their final look at the spectacular view before them. Behind them, a distance up the slope, came a sharp crack of a stick and some rustling noises. Jim sprang to his feet, Laura right beside him. Laura quickly covered Jim's mouth with her hand. She knew instinctively that he was about to call out Alex's name.

Laura whispered, "Whatever just made that noise, it's too big to be Alex."

It was almost more than Laura could stand not to call out Alex's name, but her sharp instincts told her she was correct in her assumption. Again, they heard more cracking, and the rustling sounds grew closer. They looked at each other, trying to decide if they should just stand there or try to hide. Then, through the mystery of sound travel on a mountainside, Laura picked up on the sound of voices accompanying the rustles of leaves and branches.

They both sighed in relief. At least whatever was approaching them wasn't a large animal, such as a bear or wildcat that could have potentially been a threat. As the voices approached, the couple stood their ground expectantly, waiting to see who else might be sharing the solitude of the mountain.

Two men approached through the underbrush, each dressed in a heavy hunting jacket and a matching camouflaged cap. They were both carrying shotguns that resembled Civil War relics. Laura picked up on the fact that the men were not surprised at all by their presence. The men walked up to

Jim and Laura after exchanging knowing looks, the expressions on their faces set and determined, as if they were both on an important mission.

"Howdy, strangers," the taller and older of the two men said in a tinny, nasal voice. He didn't smile, but he didn't seem hostile. Laura immediately noticed the weathered and wrinkled look of his skin, the stained and imperfect teeth, and the unshaven, scruffy look of his face.

"Long way from home, aren't ya?" he inquired.

Jim made no move to introduce himself or shake his hand, a habit that always precluded a meeting back at home.

"We were camping here last night, and our dog ran off. You haven't seen a golden retriever in your travels, have you?" Jim asked politely but with a standoffish air.

"No, can't say as we have," the first man replied, looking at his partner and then back at Jim.

The other man scrutinized Laura and then Jim. He appeared to be about their age, but his skin was already leathery with exposure to the elements, and his bent frame seemed malnourished. Laura didn't allow her gaze to focus on the men, although she could sense the younger one staring at her. She knew from experience it was best to let Jim do the talking and for her to just stand there and stare at the ground.

"You two don't come round these parts too often, I reckon," the older man continued.

"No, like I said before, we were just camping here one night," Jim replied.

"You got any kin in these parts?"

"No, but I used to come camping here on this mountain when I was a Boy Scout," Jim answered.

This obviously struck a humorous note. The two men looked at each other and burst out laughing. The older man ended the laughter with a fit of coughing. He cleared his throat and spit a wad of mucus off to one side.

Even staring at the ground, Laura could sense the palpable irritation emanating from Jim. She imagined that if she had looked at him, she would have seen his face redden in anger.

Before Jim responded, the older man spoke. "Funny thing, we both been out here searching for something too. We been lookin' for the men who been tyin' red flags to the trees on our mountain."

"Your mountain?" Jim asked with interest.

"Seems as though just cause we are a little behind in some property taxes there's these men who think we gotta sell this mountain to them. They want to take away our huntin' grounds and build some big fancy-ass resort."

The man stepped closer to Jim and looked him in the eyes, his gun cradled tightly against his chest. "Now that don't seem quite fair, does it? We been tendin' to this mountain for generations, and now, just because someone wants a pretty view from their window, they think they got a right to it."

Jim didn't respond to the comment. He took Laura's arm and backed a step away from the stranger.

"I would really love to chat with you, but we need to look for our dog and head back to our car," Jim stated matter-of-factly.

"You sure you ain't seen no men with red flags?" the man asked again. "I hear they're in season," he said, raising his gun and holding it up in front of him. The two men burst into another fit of laughter.

Laura wondered if they had already been hitting the moonshine. Thanks to the crisp mountain air, she couldn't smell the stench of their breath. Laura was all too familiar with the smell of alcohol on a man's breath first thing in the morning.

"No, we haven't seen anyone else out here." Jim turned and pulled Laura back toward their packs. Laura could feel the stares of the men burning through her back. She was glad that she was dressed in thick clothing that avoided attracting attention to herself.

The couple loaded the packs, considerably lighter than when they traveled in, on their backs and quickly left the area, leaving the two men standing and watching them. Laura wondered how long the men had known they were there; she felt sure they had been watching them for more than that morning. She recalled the silence of the forest and wondered if the men had been lurking around their campsite all night, the hush from the wildlife a sign of their presence. She suddenly had the sick feeling that maybe they were the reason Alex had not returned. Good quality, well-bred hunting dogs like Goldens were a hot commodity in these parts. She dispelled the thought and kept the hope alive that Alex had merely wandered off and was, even now, waiting for them back at the car.

On the return hike, Jim was intensely quiet. Laura waited for him to resume the search as he had promised, but instead he bore forward at a rapid pace and didn't even turn around to see if Laura was following. He never once mentioned looking for Alex. Laura sensed that if she called the dog's name it would set Jim off in a rage. Laura could tell he had been deeply insulted by the meeting with the two men. Because they had the guns, they had maintained the upper hand in the conversation. Laura felt sure things would have gone differently if the locals had not been carrying loaded weapons.

They reached the trailhead in half the time it took them to make the journey into the woods. The day was still young, but Laura knew better than to ask Jim to linger and search for Alex. When they were in sight of the car, Laura jogged past Jim and frantically searched the immediate area. She called Alex's name and even studied the ground around the car. Her heart melted when she saw the footprints Alex had made when the three of them were tumbling on the ground before their hike a day ago, but she didn't see any fresh prints.

Jim arrived and walked straight to the trunk without helping Laura in her search. "He's not here. Let's go home," Jim said abruptly.

"Look, Jim, I'm sorry those men upset you, but please remember how important it is to me to find Alex."

"There is a time to cut your losses and move on, Laura. Now is that time. I'll get you another damn dog that looks just like that one."

Laura stopped, absolutely stunned by Jim's stinging words.

"Is that all you think he was to me, just some pet?" Laura asked weakly, on the verge of tears.

Jim looked at her as he opened the trunk and removed his pack from his back. "Am I supposed to believe that he was some integral part of your life and that you can't live without him? He was just a dog, Laura. I liked him too, but he is replaceable. You can't accuse me of not doing my best to find him. Looking for him ruined our entire damn trip!"

"I can't believe you just said that," she replied in almost a whisper, not able to hold back the tears any longer. "Do you remember the reason you got me the dog in the first place? You are the one who opened the door for me to fall in love with him. Love isn't something you can turn on and off like a switch. Just because he wasn't a person does not change the fact that I did—I do—love him very much," she answered, tears rolling down her cheeks.

"I got the dog for you as a companion. He is not a person, for God's sake," Jim argued.

"And you honestly think that getting me another puppy will make everything all better?"

"I didn't say that. Now you are putting words in my mouth. I just don't think we are going to find the dog, so if you get another one, it will help ease the pain of losing this one."

"Why don't you really ease my pain and let me get pregnant?" Laura blurted out before she could help herself.

Jim stopped packing and slammed the hood of the trunk. Laura immediately regretted her comment, but now that she had brought up the subject she wasn't going to back down. For a brief moment, she thought about apologizing and telling Jim she didn't mean what she had just said, but she couldn't bring herself to do it. She did mean what she had just said, and she yearned for a chance at motherhood. It was probably the only thing that could fill the void from losing her dog.

"Laura," Jim started, "I didn't want to have to tell you this, in this way. I can't have children. I had a vasectomy when I was twenty-five. I knew I didn't want kids. Being single, I didn't want to take the chance of creating an unwanted pregnancy."

Laura felt as if she had just been punched in the stomach. She doubled over and sat down hard on the ground. She placed her head on her knees and began to sob.

Jim approached and knelt down, placing his hands on the back of her head. "Until I met you, and fell in love with you, I really didn't think I wanted any children. You changed all that. I didn't know how to tell you about the operation. I guess I always figured if we wanted children badly enough there were other ways of having them—you know, sperm banks, adoption."

Laura had the feeling that all the comforts and joys of the marriage had just been pulled out from under her like a rug. She simply couldn't understand how Jim could have been deceiving her all this time, acting like having a child was just a matter of timing.

She looked up at Jim and through her tears said, "Let's go."

"We can discuss this on the ride home," Jim directed.

He helped Laura to her feet and took her pack. He threw it in the back of the car and climbed in the driver's side. Laura wordlessly got in the passenger side.

"I know this has been a rough weekend for you, but part of life is dealing with the not-so-pleasant aspects. You will always encounter them, but how you deal with them is what determines your moral fiber."

"Please don't lecture me on dealing with the more unpleasant aspects of life," Laura said through clenched teeth. "Right now I consider your deceit an unpleasant aspect, and I'm not quite sure how I am going to deal with it."

Jim started the car and made a U-turn, spitting rocks out from under the tires as he gunned the engine. Laura felt the car slow down immediately and knew that Jim had only slowed down for fear he might mark up the paint on the BMW. She noticed he drove more carefully down the dirt road and back onto the main highway. He didn't comment on Laura's statement. The pair rode in silence for a while.

Finally Laura asked, "So is this your idea of discussing the situation?"

"You are obviously too upset to be rational. I think it is better if we wait until you calm down."

"And don't you think I have a reason to be upset?" Laura asked with anger in her voice for the first time in their marriage. "In the course of one weekend I lose my dog, find out my husband is extorting land from a long generation of landowners, and that he lied to me about having children. I think that constitutes a right to be a bit upset."

"Don't blow things out of proportion, Laura. Yes, you did lose your dog, but we are proceeding in a lawful manner to obtain the property from those people. And I explained to you why I didn't tell you I couldn't have children. There are other ways of conceiving children," Jim defended himself.

"Everything is so cut and dried for you, isn't it, Jim? If it can be figured out on paper and voted on, then that makes it ethical and practical. You never seem to look at the moral sides of any issue."

"Are you calling me immoral? I didn't seem so immoral to you when I asked you to marry me and took you from poverty into a life of luxury."

"So now you are accusing me of marrying you for your money?" Laura asked defensively.

"I'm just saying that I'm the same person now that you married then, and you didn't seem to mind me when it made a difference in your lifestyle."

Laura felt bile rising into her throat. Never had she been so insulted in her whole life, not since she had endured her painful childhood and adults had treated her no better than one of their animals. Now that she was an adult, she didn't have to take this kind of abuse.

"Stop the car," she demanded.

"What the hell do you mean, stop the car?"

"You heard me. Stop the damn car!"

Jim heard the anger seething in her voice and tried to placate her.

"Don't be ridiculous, Laura. We are fifty miles from home. Wait until we get home. Then you can be angry and walk out on me if that makes you feel better."

Laura waited until Jim braked for a curve and then threw the passenger door open.

"What are you doing?" Jim yelled, veering the car toward the shoulder and skidding on the loose stones as he quickly applied the brakes.

Before the car was completely stopped, Laura launched herself out onto the grassy bank. She rolled a few times but recovered her balance and got to her feet. Uninjured, she turned and sprinted into the woods beside the road. She heard a car door slam and Jim call her name from the roadside. She knew he would not pursue her. It was too important that he return home and get prepared for his big meeting. She immediately regretted not grabbing her backpack on her exit from the car. Laura stood still in the woods for a moment and listened. Soon enough she heard tires turning up loose stones as Jim peeled away in anger back onto the highway.

Standing still, undecided and confused, she started to notice the sounds in the forest around her: the distant caws of crows calling to one another from high treetops, a gentle breeze rustling the leaves in the trees. Small animals scurried about the forest, making tiny crackling and rustling noises. The sounds drifted toward her like a gentle rain shower on a summer day. The forest suddenly came to life for her as it had during her childhood.

Laura headed back toward the road, formulating a plan as she went. Her heart was numb from being broken into a thousand pieces in the matter of two days, but her mind was racing with a plan to remove herself from her present predicament. Above all else, Laura was a survivor. She had clawed and climbed her way out of oblivion and poverty. Such a feat left a person with certain adaptive skills in difficult situations. Laura had no one to blame but herself for this particular predicament. She had followed Jim like a lamb to slaughter without putting up the least bit of resistance to his dominating charm. No one had forced her into this relationship, and now it was up to her to figure a way out. She recalled the old saying, "If it seems to be too good to be true, it probably is." For the first time in over a year, Laura began thinking for herself. She noted that it felt really good.

# Chapter 7

In sight of the highway but still hidden from people passing down the road, Laura found a soft patch of dry grass and sat down. Everything was happening so quickly that she needed time to sort out her thoughts and make some decisions. As with any major decision, Laura knew that she had to review her options and then decide which one made the most sense. Right now, anger was directing her actions, and she knew that was a bad thing. Angry people tended to act irrationally, she knew from experience. If she acted irrationally, then there was a chance she would only make the situation worse by making poor decisions. If that happened, she could very likely end up back on her own again with nowhere to go.

Laura looked around her to get a bearing on her location. She had heard Jim mention that they were about fifty miles from home. The sun was only inches above the horizon, which meant that she had only a few hours of daylight left. Straightening her legs so she could reach in her jeans pockets, Laura searched them to see if she had inadvertently left any money in them after shopping for supplies Friday night. Coming up empty, she remembered she had put all her money on her dresser at home, knowing she wouldn't have a need for it on a wilderness camping trip. She took stock of what she knew about her situation: it was almost dark; she had no money, no food, no shelter; and she was a long way from home. Her choices were to hitchhike home and face Jim or spend the night in the woods and make her way home tomorrow when Jim would be at work or in a meeting. Or was there somewhere else she could go and seek refuge for an evening? There wasn't a single person she felt comfortable enough to confide in, never mind show up at their door and ask for lodging. Relatives were out of the question. There was only one surviving aunt whom she felt at all close to during her childhood—her mother's sister—and Laura hadn't spoken to her since she had run away from home many years ago.

Laura stood up and looked back into the woods where she had come from. Suddenly, a sense of déjà vu swept over her like a cold wave. She was ten years old again. Her dad was drunk and screaming at her mother. She knew the beating would begin, so she fled out of the house and into the woods surrounding their mountain shack. She stood there, just like she was standing here now, fraught with indecision. She could spend the night in the woods, cold, alone, and hungry, or return to the house and suffer the wrath of her father. Only once did she make the decision to return to the house, and the things that happened to her that night made this decision seem simple.

Laura wrapped her arms around herself and, seeing herself as that ten-year-old child, she wandered into the forest. The setting sun no longer reached the forest floor, and shadows seemed to creep up from the ground and envelop the forest in a blanket of darkness. She'd always had a favorite spot beneath a ledge in the forest at home that she would curl herself into, dry leaves her only bedding. She remembered the feeling of waking up in the morning and pulling the insects and debris from her tangled hair. She searched the forest now, half expecting to see the ledge of rock that she had cowered under as a child. She walked until the forest was overtaken by blackness and she could no longer see her way to navigate through the trees. She walked into several branches. As they swiped her face, she felt the sharp branches tear at her tender skin. She reached up to her face and felt a warm, sticky area on her cheek that she knew must be blood. Unable to see any longer, shivering in the chill of the night air, Laura got down on her hands and knees and felt her way to the base of a large tree. The groundcover under the tree was soft and loamy and smelled familiarly of earth and fall leaves. Like a small animal burrowing, Laura curled into a tight ball and swept the leaves and groundcover around her body. She tried to hang on to reality, but exhaustion took over, and she drifted into a restless sleep. Sleeping in the woods triggered memories of her past. In her dream, she returned to the shack she grew up in on the night she ran away from home.

She felt the physical pain of tripping over the gas can and then the emotional pain of seeing her mother's twisted and lifeless arm hanging over the side of the bed. She stood up and grabbed the rusty handle of the gas can and turned to look back at the shack. She had heard her father bellow after she unlatched the door, and she expected to see his hulking black silhouette in the doorway at any moment. She shivered in the cold night air, barefoot, dressed in only a nightgown and robe. Her spare hand reached into her bathrobe pocket and felt for the pack of matches she had used to light the candles earlier that night. How ironic that the matches were her only possession; she was standing there with enough fuel to end all the horrors she had known throughout her childhood. Seconds ticked by as fate, destiny—whatever force drives a person to make an impulsive decision—took hold of Laura. It seemed the entire universe paused, waiting for her decision so it could start rolling down whichever path Laura would choose. It took all of her strength and willpower to turn her feet back in the direction of the shack. If her father came through that door before she finished her task, she felt quite sure he would kill her. She left the next few minutes in the hands of fate and decided that maybe death would be a good alternative to living life without her mother. She sprinted up the steps and struggled with the cap on the spout of the rusty can, its contents sloshing wildly, as if excited at the prospect of being released. It stuck, refusing to cooperate with her cold fingers, slippery from nervous sweat. Finally, the cap rotated and fell to the wooden porch floor, and Laura spilled the contents of the can in a puddle next to the door and then backed down the stairs and away from the porch, leaving a trail of fuel.

When she had backed a safe distance from the porch, she ran back up and placed the half-empty can in the puddle next to the door. Every breath she took was painful from the fumes of the gas and the expectation that at any second her father was going to burst through the door. Just as she set the can down, she heard her father's footsteps approaching the doorway, the heavy clomping of his boots unsteady but determined. She heard angry words but could not make out what he was saying. She bolted back down the stairs and almost didn't turn back because of her fear. The universe halted once again. She had a decision to make: face her father or run in fear forever and let the horrible man get away with the murder and abuse he had caused her and her mother. Twenty feet from the shack, she willed herself to stop and turn back toward the doorway. Her mind screamed at her to keep running, but her heart stopped her feet cold in their tracks.

Just as she turned to face the shack, her father burst unsteadily through the doorway, catching himself on the doorframe so as not to lose his balance and fall forward. He glared at her and spoke his final words to his waif of a daughter as she faced him: judge, jury, and executioner.

# Chapter 8

LAURA FORCED HERSELF TO WAKE up out of the dream and then immediately drifted back into some unconscious state the mind enters when trying to protect the body. Her mind drifted away from the scene with her father, like a soft, fluffy cloud drifts through the summer sky. Wrapped in a mental cocoon, Laura's mind released her spirit, and she floated away from her body. She rose above herself and saw her cold, curled shell lying on the dark ground at the base of the tree. She stayed there a moment and saw her body taking slow, rhythmic breaths and wondered what purpose there was to returning to such a fragile form, which seemed so prone to injury and pain. Her spirit finally took her away from her body, traveling at lightning speed through the tops of the trees and back toward the mountains. It was as if she were being called to go there, some other spirit now guiding her. Suddenly there was a transition that Laura didn't quite understand. She seemed to be running now, although she didn't quite know how that was possible. She sensed her closeness to the ground and felt powerful legs propelling her with ease through thickets and over rocky terrain. She smelled scents that were so powerful they seized her mind and sent her into shivers of delight. The form soon arrived at a familiar area, and it slowed down to investigate. She realized with a shock that she was seeing the outcropping of rock where she and Jim had camped. In the moonlight, the vessel continued forward and sniffed the now-cold embers of the fire, the ground where their tent had been, and even a nearby spruce, where the smell of urine tainted the lower boughs. She sensed a longing in the vessel, an ache to find the life forms that offered it food, protection, and a sense of love and well-being.

The vessel turned and bolted off toward the scents of things that were present, things that were alive, things that would run when he chased them and offer food if he could catch them. As the vessel gained speed, Laura sensed an increase in the speed of her own consciousness, a ripping, almost tearing sensation as she drifted upward and back toward the treetops. She somehow knew that this presence could also sense her. Then he stopped and stared at the air above him. She watched once again from above as he sat down and whined, cocked his head, and barked into the dark emptiness that surrounded him. Realizing that whatever had been with him was now gone, he bounded forward and continued his search for those living things that tantalized and drew him back to a wild and free state. Laura knew he felt comforted and relieved by the visit and believed that life was as it should be.

Once again, Laura hovered over her own body, peering down at her fragile form. She had a decision to make. She had a strong urge not to reenter her body and continue the life search, endure the tragedy and failure that accompanied that stage of existence. However, there was some compelling reason that she must return and resume her role. She knew not what that purpose was or who was telling her there were still unfulfilled parts of her life for which she must provide closure. She just knew. She then had a feeling of peace, of sleepiness, even a certain sense of resolution, as she drifted like a floating leaf falling from a tree, back into her body.

The first shards of sunlight filtered through the leaves of the trees above her. It was not the sunlight that woke Laura but the cacophony of birdsongs resounding from every piece of foliage in the forest. Flocks of birds swarmed into the area and tried their best to outsing other flocks of birds that occupied the same territory. Single birds, roosting high in the treetops, sang in their loudest voices over the din of the flocks. The result was a ruckus, the likes of which Laura had never heard before.

Cold, sore from her fall from the car, filthy with dirt, with dried blood on her face, Laura still smiled as she sat up. Gone was the fear of suddenly being alone and facing an unknown future. The songs of the birds seemed to lift her spirit and revive her sense of adventure. She suddenly saw life as an adventure, full of twists and turns that one can never foresee. The birds reminded her of how important freedom was. If you couldn't sing your own song, then you were no more than a prisoner, a bird in a cage. And that was exactly what her marriage to Jim had been.

However, even birds in cages need food and water. Laura had an overwhelming thirst, a burning pain in her throat that needed to be quenched. Between the hike yesterday and the trauma her body experienced fending off cold and stress, Laura was dangerously near dehydration. She stood and felt a bit dizzy for a second. Bracing herself against the tree, she waited for the feeling to pass. She glanced at the woods around her and wondered how far she had wandered from the road last evening.

She looked down at her soiled and torn clothing and felt her hair, matted with leaves and small twigs. She needed to find some water and then search for a way home. *Home,* she thought. That word seemed empty when referring to her condo with Jim. Now that seemed more like a temporary phase of life that had come and gone and held both pleasant and unpleasant memories. It was not a place that she could respond to like a home, where one felt comfort and love. But she knew she had to return there, if only to get her clothes and some money and find resolution to her marriage with Jim.

Instead of heading back in the direction she thought the road would be, Laura headed deeper into the woods in hopes of finding a source of water. She knew that if she got in trouble this far into the woods, her chances of rescue were zero. No one would find her body, except maybe a hunter who would stumble upon it sometime in the future. She could see the news headlines: MAN FINDS HUMAN REMAINS DURING HUNTING TRIP. *An unidentified body was found yesterday by what investigators believe are the remains of a female that could be related to a rape and murder case several years ago.* No one would suspect some chick jumped out of a moving vehicle under her own power and wandered into the woods until she died of thirst. Still, Laura's instincts told her that she would find water in this direction. She followed a gentle downward ravine, which usually indicated that water had carved a path out of the mountain. Usually a river or stream could be found at the base.

Stumbling now, willing her body to take each step forward, Laura began to doubt that she would ever see another living soul again. Her lips were cracked from exposure and lack of moisture. She no longer had enough saliva to wet them and ease the intense burning. Her tongue felt swollen, like a thick cotton washcloth stuffed in her mouth. Her body kept tempting her to sit down and rest, but Laura's will kept moving her forward. It was her only chance of surviving this ordeal. Laura noticed a very subtle change in the terrain. The trees began to turn from a large spruce variety into smaller, thinner softwoods. That was a good sign. The ground beneath her began to slope more abruptly, and before long she could hear the soft gurgling of a nearby stream.

Laura's heart raced. She was so happy she would have cried tears of joy if there had been one ounce of fluid in her body to spare. She ran forward, feeling the waves of exhaustion trying to pull her down. Her feet felt as if they had lead weights tied to them, but she rhythmically picked each foot up and forced herself to jog forward. She couldn't see the stream yet, but she could smell the aroma of the musky, wet earth around the stream as one can smell the salty ocean air before the ocean is visible. A large branchy bush blocked her view of the stream, and she grabbed it and pulled it aside.

*Almost there*, she thought to herself, preparing to burst through the brush and drink to her heart's content. But what she saw in the next instant froze her in her tracks. A black bear that apparently claimed this part of the river as his fishery was absorbed in retrieving his meal. He looked up at Laura as she pulled back the branches to reveal herself, his eyes glaring, his snout dripping with water from plunging his face into the water to find fish. Less than twenty feet apart, Laura and the bear froze, trying to decide what to do about each other. Laura was not particularly afraid of black bears. As a child she had seen many of them raiding the local garbage dumps and sometimes even their own trash cans. Her father had shot them, and she had even eaten their meat.

What remained to be known was the age, sex, and hunger status of the bear. If it was a female finding food for her cubs, Laura could be in trouble. The males were less aggressive if not particularly hungry and a lot less dangerous. Of course, she had no way of determining those facts at the moment, so she searched the surrounding bank for signs of a cub. Seeing none, she formulated her plan. Meanwhile, the bear moved cautiously to the other side of the bank and paced back and forth, as if challenging her to come into his river. Laura was not in the mood to wait the bear out, and she expected him to leave at his own leisurely pace. She needed a drink. However, she didn't feel physically strong enough to protect herself if it came to outrunning or trying to defend herself against a bear. She needed a plan; she needed to use her brain and superior intellect to outsmart the bear.

Remembering the stories from *Reader's Digest* about bear attacks, she thought she recalled the fact that bears, if challenged, will sometimes back off. Running away from them was what drew them to pursue a human. Hoping that the *Reader's Digest* had done their homework, she snapped off a branch from the bush next to her. Brandishing the branch in front of her, she decided the bear might pick up on her desperation and back down from this crazed and violent human. Mustering up the last vestiges of her strength, Laura charged down the bank into the river, screaming like a banshee and waving the branch in front of her. These actions took the bear by surprise, and he retreated farther up the bank, away from the river. Once Laura had the bear on the run, she took full advantage and continued into the stream after him. The bear paused a moment and looked behind him, apparently wondering what type of creature was chasing him. Then he lumbered off into the woods, crying his bearish cries, which sounded like a distraught child running to Mom to complain about an abusive sibling.

Laura sank to her knees in the middle of the stream. The icy water reached her waist, and the coldness took her breath away. She brought her face down to the water and plunged her whole head into the rushing current. Raising herself up, she cupped her hands and brought the life-giving liquid to her parched lips. She took great gulps of the water. It tasted a bit like algae and had a slightly fishy tang, but it seemed at that moment more delightful and refreshing than a bottled of chilled Perrier. Her stomach cramped at first from the invasion of the ice-cold liquid. She took a few deep breaths and let her system adjust to the sudden rehydration, and then she continued to take deep gulps of water. Realizing that the cold water was instantly chilling her, she stood erect and walked back to the bank.

The sun was beginning to warm the air. Laura felt the wet clothes sucking the heat from her tired body. She removed them and lay against the bank, soaking in the warm rays of the sun. Afraid that the bear might return, Laura sat up and got to work. First, she rinsed out her soiled clothes and wrung them out as much as possible. She spread the clothes on a bush to begin drying them in the sun and gentle breeze. Next, she waded back into the water and dipped her head down to the water's surface. Using her hands, she washed her matted hair in the current. Her feet and hands became numb, so she retreated back to the warm, dark soil along the bank and let herself dry off and warm up. She ran her fingers through her hair to detangle it and regain some normalcy to her appearance.

The thirst crisis over, Laura turned her thoughts to getting back to her condo. She would give herself and her clothes about an hour to dry, knowing her jeans and light jacket would never dry in that amount of time. Hopefully, the walk back toward the road and her body heat would speed up the process. She desperately wanted to get back to the condo, collect her things, and be gone before Jim returned from work.

Laura dozed lazily, regaining her strength, until she believed an hour had passed. She nibbled on a few plants around the stream she knew were edible and chewed on a pine needle to freshen her breath. She struggled back into her damp clothing and smoothed her hair with her fingers. Taking one final drink from the stream, she silently thanked the bear for allowing her to share his stream, and then she headed back the way she had come.

Laura uneventfully found her way back to the road. She was proud of her innate sense of direction and her ability to navigate through the woods. Now the trick was to try to hitchhike back to town. She paused a moment before stepping onto the shoulder of the road, realizing that she would rather face a bear and a night alone in the woods than she would ask a stranger for a ride. She began walking.

She wished she was close enough to just hike home, but she realized that if she was going to follow her agenda, she needed a speedier mode of transportation. Several cars passed her, but she couldn't find the nerve to turn toward them and stick up her thumb. She was just about to take a deep breath and solicit the next passing vehicle when she saw a dark blue Ford truck and silver horse trailer pulled along the shoulder about a half a mile up the road. Jogging slowly, Laura stole up to the back of the trailer to assess the situation.

"Will you knock it off, you stupid animal?" A man's voice seemed to come from under the trailer.

She heard a steady banging, and again the man's voice shouted, "I told you to knock it off!"

Peering around the side of the trailer, Laura saw a man kneeling beside the trailer, tightening the lug nut on what appeared to be a replacement tire. Inside the trailer, one of the two horses was pawing at the floorboards, apparently eager to disembark now that the trailer had stopped.

The man looked up, surprised to see Laura come into view around the back of the trailer.

"It's all right, ma'am," the man said politely. "I have everything under control. It is just a flat tire. I almost have the spare on."

Laura smiled and tried to decide how to broach the subject that she was there because she needed help, not the other way around. The man stood up and wiped his greasy hands on his jeans and gave Laura a scrutinizing look. She realized her appearance was less than presentable. She was probably sending all kinds of red flags up in the man's mind.

"I didn't even hear your car pull up. Do you have one of those hybrids that sneak up on people? Blind people hate those cars, you know."

"Actually, I came on foot. I was not driving a car," Laura replied.

The man stood there a moment with a puzzled expression on his face. He crossed his arms and stared at Laura, waiting for her to explain herself. Laura, on the other hand, was busy with her own thoughts, trying to decide if she should spill her guts and tell the truth of the situation or make up a story.

Before either could speak, a crashing noise came from the trailer. "Damn it!" The man spoke in obvious distress. He ripped open the side door of the trailer, and Laura rushed behind him to see the cause of the clatter. Apparently, the horse that had been pawing had reared up, trying to exit the trailer in his own way, and its front leg now rested over the front chest bar. The horse began violently struggling, trying to propel itself backward and pull its leg back over the bar, unable to do so because of the confines of the trailer.

"Whoa, buddy, now just calm down, and we'll get you out of here."

Laura watched the man slowly approach the horse, afraid that any quick movement would cause the horse to resume struggling. Again, the horse panicked and with frenzied efforts tried to free its leg from the divider. Once it stopped struggling, the man reached carefully to pull the pin that released the bar and would free the horse's leg. Unfortunately, the weight of the animal's body on the bar froze the pin fast in its moorings.

"Damn it to hell, now what do I do?" the man said, for the first time sounding a bit panicked.

"Maybe I could lift the horse's leg up enough to allow you to get the pin out," Laura volunteered.

"No, that wouldn't work. The horse has his full body weight on that leg, and there is no way even the two of us could lift it up. I have some tranquilizer in the truck, and I think we need to calm him down before we can accomplish anything."

As the man stepped away from the horse, the horse began another frenzied attempt to free itself, pinning the man inside. Laura stepped back from the trailer door, covering her ears against the explosive noises coming from the struggling horse trying to battle its way to freedom. Twelve hundred pounds of struggling, terrified animal sounded like it had the power to pound the trailer to pieces. As Laura stood there, she noticed the chock the man had used to change the trailer tire. It was a long, slanted block about a foot high with a flat top that allowed a person to drive the trailer up on it and lift the tire on the other side off the ground without having to use a jack. Without thinking of the consequences, Laura grabbed the chock and ran back to the trailer door. Inside, the man was pinned against the wall while the horse thrashed inches in front of his face. He saw Laura out of the corner of his eye and stared in disbelief as she placed herself in extreme danger of being crushed by the horse.

Laura's instincts told her that if she got the chock under the horse's free front foot when it reared up, it would elevate the horse enough to either take the weight off the bar or allow the horse to free himself. At the moment the horse reared again, Laura crawled under the divider and placed the chock in the location she thought the horse would land. She prayed she'd placed it in the right spot and that the horse would not injure itself further by landing partially on it, making the situation even worse.

As quick as lightning, Laura pulled her body back under the divider. The horse's foot cascaded back down and landed squarely and firmly on the chock. The horse immediately felt the strength of his new position and within seconds had successfully pulled its leg over the divider. It stood there for a moment, quaking, one foot still elevated on the chock, as if he were waiting for a pedicure.

For a moment the man stood in shock and disbelief. Laura stared back and shrugged. "Well, it worked, didn't it?" she replied to his, "Are you crazy lady?" stare.

"Do you realize you could have been killed?" the man chided.

"Look, mister, I have had several near-death experiences in the last forty-eight hours, and this one was no more spectacular than the rest."

The man patted the horse and talked quietly to it, trying to calm its quaking body. He carefully reached under the divider and pulled the horse's leg forward at the knee, lifting it so he could remove the chock. He then carefully set the horse's leg down. Standing up slowly, so as not to frighten the animal, he handed the chock out the door to Laura. He repositioned the hay bag so the horse could reach it. The other horse continued to eat its own hay, seemingly unaffected by all the commotion. The frightened horse reached his neck forward and took a few nervous bites of hay. Laura could tell that the horse was eating not out of hunger but in order to perform some natural function that would calm his frazzled nerves. He would chew a few bites, stop, and look around, seemingly on edge again, and then lunge for another bite of hay before the first one had been fully chewed.

Laura's own stomach growled with the hunger pangs that had been growing steadily stronger by the hour.

The man backed out of the trailer door and quietly, slowly, closed the latch.

"He'll be all right now. I'm sure he learned a lot from that experience. He'll wait until I open the door before he tries to make his own exit. Of course there is the danger he might bolt out backward when I open the back door to unload him, but I guess I'll cross that bridge when I come to it."

The man then stuck out his hand and introduced himself. "I would like to know the name of the brave lady who risked her neck for that crazy horse. My name is Nick. Nick Jackson."

Laura stood there holding the chock, and Nick reached over and took it from her grasp before extending his hand again.

For the first time Laura studied his face. By the time she responded and took his hand in hers, she had noticed the kindness of his eyes. They were pale green, with a hint of gray. His tousled brown hair was a bit on the long side and had a clean but unkempt look. His face was stubby with five o'clock shadow. He appeared very tired.

"My name is Laura. Nice to meet you, Nick."

For some reason, maybe because her identity was in the process of changing, she didn't offer her last name.

"I owe you big time, Laura. You did a brave thing back there. Not only was it quick and intelligent thinking, it was extremely brave as well."

Laura felt herself blush. She couldn't remember ever being complimented on her intelligence and bravery before. She'd simply acted on impulse, nothing more.

"How can I ever repay you?" Nick asked genuinely.

Laura felt less afraid of the situation than when she first approached to ask for a ride, so she blurted out the truth. Part of it, anyway.

"I've had a really lousy weekend," she started. "I lost my dog, got lost in the woods, and nearly died of thirst. I ditched my ride home because of, shall we say, an extreme difference of opinion."

She felt she'd covered the gist of the situation without revealing too many personal facts.

"The truth is," she continued, "I need to get home, and I don't have a ride. You can see for yourself that I am not in much condition to be asking strangers for rides. And I am absolutely starving, so if you have any food in the truck and are willing to share, I am about to chew my own arm off."

Nick smiled gently. She could tell his smile was genuine.

"Laura, I would be honored to give you a ride home. It is the least I can do for such heroic efforts."

Nick turned his back on her for a moment and collected his tools from fixing the tire. He rolled the flat to the back of his pickup and heaved it in the bed, along with his tools. He walked to the passenger-side door and opened it for Laura. Nick walked around, got in, and started the truck. The powerful diesel roared to life as soon as the glow plug light was off. Nick reached next to him and grabbed a bag of chips and tossed them to Laura.

"It isn't much, but have at it. Just how long has it been since you've eaten a meal?" Nick inquired.

Laura thought for a moment. "I guess it was breakfast yesterday." Yesterday morning seemed like an eternity away when she thought about it.

"I wish I had more to feed you, but I don't, unless you eat hay. I do have a thermos of coffee here." He reached under the seat and pulled out a red thermos. Laura accepted it gratefully and poured some steaming coffee into the lid.

"One more question. I need to know your address so I can take you home."

Laura typed the address into his GPS. She secretly wished they were farther from her home than they were. The GPS showed an arrival time of just under an hour. She would have liked to sit in the comfort of the truck for several hours rather than go back and face her future. After Nick pulled the trailer out onto the highway and eased up to highway speed, the two made idle conversation about horses and unimportant subjects like traffic and weather. Laura devoured the entire bag of chips and drank the rest of the coffee.

Before the hour was up, the truck and trailer pulled into the development that Laura had called home. She asked Nick to let her off at the entrance. She didn't want anyone she knew to see her getting out of a pickup truck with a strange man, and she knew the horse trailer was sure to attract attention. She was also afraid Nick would have trouble turning around in the narrow drive, which wasn't meant for trucks with trailers.

As Laura thanked Nick profusely, he reached into his jeans pocket and pulled out his wallet. He opened it, extracted a business card, and handed it to Laura, who took it with a certain curiosity.

"This has my name and address on it. I know we just met, but I have a sixth sense about you. I feel as if you need a friend. I feel that someday our paths may cross again. Take that, for whatever it's worth."

"Thank you, "Laura repeated for the third time. "You've helped me out more than you can imagine."

Laura glanced at the card, which read NICHOLAS JACKSON, DVM. It included his address and his office and cell numbers. He specialized in horses and large animals. Laura closed the heavy door to the pickup and stood watching as the rig made a clean U-turn in the wide entrance of the development and then headed back down the road. Laura waved as Nick passed, and Nick responded with a wave of his own. Laura sighed, turned, and walked down the sidewalk toward the condo. She felt very tired and very hungry.

# Chapter 9

LAURA TAPPED THE NUMBERS INTO the condo lock, thankful to have keyless entry. Relieved that getting into the condo was easy and uneventful, Laura first headed into the kitchen to grab something to eat. On the counter lay a note from Jim. Not ready to read it, Laura rustled up the ingredients for a sandwich, prepared it, and ate it with gusto. It had been many years since she had felt such hunger pangs. She poured a glass of juice to wash down the sandwich and braced herself to read Jim's note.

Laura,

I hope your foolishness has taught you a lesson. I knew you would find your way home, and I'm glad you chose to come back when I was not here. I think we both need some time away from each other. If you want to work things out, I am willing to forgive your behavior. I know you are just hurting right now. Why don't you take the credit card and go on vacation for a week? By that time, my deal will hopefully be sealed and we will both have the edge taken off our anger. I do want to apologize for the timing of the news about my lack of being able to father a child, but I am not going to apologize for having the operation. I did what I thought was right at the time, and I am still not convinced I even want to have children. I am just being honest with you so when you come back all the cards are on the table. I am willing to get you another dog.

Take care of yourself.

Jim

Laura read the note again and stared at it in disbelief. This note was proof that Jim would take no credit for their disagreement. He believed that Laura was to blame for this entire situation. True, the series of events leading up to Alex's disappearance was no one's fault, but had he shown a little more compassion and understanding, she would have never left like she did. And how about his remark that she married him for his money? That was absolutely uncalled-for.

Laura huffed into the bedroom, peeling off her still-damp clothing. She realized now that she must have smelled like pond scum to Nick and had probably left damp marks on his truck seat. It felt extremely wonderful to remove the wet, stinky clothes that she had been wearing for two days. If not worried about dirtying the sheets, she would have crawled into the bed that very moment and taken a nap. But she knew she would enjoy the hot shower the moment she got in, and she did. She stood, letting the pelting flow of hot water soothe her tensions away, forgetting for the first time to feel self-conscious in the glass shower stall. She directed the spray on the back of her neck and massaged the muscles in her neck and shoulders.

When her skin turned the pinkish color of a partially cooked lobster, she decided it was time to get out. She dried herself with the luxurious cotton towel and wrapped her hair up in a smaller one. She smelled like clean soap and fragrant flowers from her botanical conditioner. She sat on the edge of the bed and noticed Alex's dog bed beside her own. Her heart broke all over again as she pictured Alex lying in his bed, staring up at her with those pleading eyes. Laura broke down as all her defenses from the last few days finally crumbled. She crawled toward her pillow and buried her face and let the tears flow. So much of her life had changed over the weekend; it was almost too much to bear. She didn't remember actually falling asleep, but it sure shocked the heck out of her when she woke up to find it dark outside.

Eyes puffy and nose stuffed from her heavy sobbing, Laura sat upright, temporarily confused by the darkness that now descended in the room. Suddenly, her heart began to race, and she began to sweat. *Oh no*, she thought. *What time is it? What time is it?* She fumbled toward the nightstand, knocking over the lamp and a book as she tried to find the clock. When she did find it, she threw the covers aside and stood up, her chest heaving as she surveyed her options. Jim could be home at any minute. Not that it would be the end of the world if they encountered one another, but leaving would just be a lot easier without him around. She sat up and pulled the towel from her hair. She had slept so soundly that the towel had stayed tightly wrapped on her head. Her hair cascaded down in wet tendrils, moist from the damp towel. She found it difficult to force herself out of her groggy state after her deep sleep.

She ran into the bathroom and quickly dried her hair but didn't bother with any makeup. She swept her toiletries into a cosmetic bag and grabbed one of Jim's favorite plush towels. She felt no guilt over taking it with her. She went into the bedroom and pulled a large suitcase out of the closet. The last time it had been used was her honeymoon. She opened the suitcase on the bed and began stuffing all the clothes she thought would fit into it. She had to sit on it in order to force it closed. She dragged it off the bed. It hit the floor with a loud thump, which scared her for a second because it sounded like a car door closing. Laura was more afraid of Jim returning than she cared to admit. She glanced around the bedroom and saw her purse on the dresser. In it were a few credit cards and some cash she knew she would need. She also made the bed. She wasn't going to degrade herself by leaving the place a wreck. Nothing in the entire townhouse had sentimental value. It was already decorated when she moved in, and the few wedding gifts she incorporated were given to them by Jim's friends and relatives. He could keep everything. She came with nothing, and she intended to leave the same way.

Satisfied that she had everything she would need, she dragged her suitcase to the garage entrance. Jim had parked her car in the garage when he had left. She muscled her suitcase into the trunk and ran back in the condo for her purse and smaller bags. When she reappeared in the garage, she used the automatic opener to raise the garage doors with and backed the BMW out with a sense of relief. She had to stop herself from flooring the car and racing away. She headed out of the development toward the highway and stopped at a diner to grab a bite to eat and think about things. She had no idea where she was going and needed to make a game plan. As she ate a quick hamburger dinner, she formulated a semblance of a plan in her mind. When she got back in the car, she looked at the gas gauge and saw that Jim had filled the tank for her. He was either really considerate or really ready to get rid of her. Laura couldn't decide which option was the truth, but she had her suspicions.

# Chapter 10

THE HIGHWAY HEADED BACK IN the direction of the Blue Ridge Mountains that Laura had been so desperate to escape that same morning. Laura felt as if time was spinning out of control. With it, her life was being sucked away in a whirlpool. If the road before her suddenly caved into a bottomless pit, she doubted she would even try to avoid it. She would feel a sense of relief driving into a blackness that would end all of her turmoil.

Laura had a big decision to make. Remembering the lack of police presence in her little town, she was not surprised that there had not been any type of in-depth investigation into her whereabouts after the death of her parents. After she left, she'd searched the papers. Sure enough, a few days later there was a small article about a man and his wife who died in a house fire. Authorities believed the fire had been started by a candle tipping over, and there was no mention of any foul play. The article stated that there was a sixteen-year-old daughter living in the home but that her remains were not found. She was being reported as a missing person. There was no mention of her aunt, her mother's only sister, who was the family's closest living relative. The next day an article appeared about a search party for the missing teen that had to be called off due to bad weather. Now, if she returned to try to find her aunt, there was danger that someone might make a connection to that event and start questioning where she had been all these years.

If her calculations were correct, the last time she had seen her aunt was fourteen years ago. She wasn't even sure she was still alive, but the woman seemed healthy fourteen years ago and should only be in her early seventies now. The poor people of the mountains didn't have the life expectancy of people with more money who could afford better diets and a less harsh lifestyle. If she was dead, at least Laura could research and find out what happened to her. She needed to have some connection with family at this point in her life. She'd spent the first twenty years of her life hating her family and running away from them, and now she found it ironic that she was so desperate to contact them. Actually, not "them." If her father had been alive, she would never go near him again, or anyone related to him. She had a great sense of sadness that she never got time to spend with her mother without the oppression and abusiveness of her father. Her mother had such a kind spirit and in her own way had tried to be a good mother, but Laura rarely had happy moments in her childhood when she could bond with her mother and they could enjoy their mother-daughter relationship. This was one reason she wanted to have children so badly. She wanted her own chance to have a family, to experience a loving family environment. Not having many existing family options to find, Laura concentrated on the one aunt who just might be alive and remember her. If she did find her, Laura was going to have a lot of explaining to do.

Laura drove for two hours before she felt fatigue overtake her. It would be difficult enough to find the town she'd lived in fourteen years ago, and she had no intention of trying to find it at night. She was sure that the town would have changed so much that she wouldn't recognize it in daylight. If she did run into someone from her past, she was quite sure no one would not recognize her as the undernourished teen they had seen so many years ago. She was also sure there was no mapping for her little town on a GPS, as the town consisted of just a few buildings and there were no crossroads or anything of significance to map.

The road narrowed into a single lane winding through the various smaller mountains that dotted the main ridge. In various locations were lookout points where motorists could stop and enjoy the view, and at several of those locations were small, shabby motels that accommodated maybe a dozen people. Laura picked the one that looked the least shabby and pulled the car into the narrow strip that served as a parking area. Many of the motels were built right onto the edge of the mountain to offer the best view of the scenery. Because of the dilapidated state of most of the lodges, a visitor might feel that at some point in the night she might find herself rolling down the side of the mountain, bed and all.

Laura checked in with her credit card and asked the desk person for some information about Rimrock, the town where she was headed. But the clerk just shook his head and said he had never heard of it. The man appeared to be ancient, and Laura wasn't sure if he really hadn't heard of it or if he didn't want to be bothered so he could get back to bed. She had roused him from a cot in a small room behind the reception area that consisted of a shabby arm chair, a TV, and a mini fridge. She got chills when she realized that at one point in her life, coming to a place like this would have seemed as elegant as staying at the Plaza would to a normal person.

She accepted her room key and walked back outside to find her room along the single strip of tiny cottages. The sharp smell of bleach invaded her nostrils before she even turned on the lights. When she did reach the lights, she saw a single bed in a small room, with an even smaller bathroom attached. *At least it's a step up from where I spent last night,* she mused to herself. She quickly changed into her nightclothes, which she had packed in a small bag so she didn't have to drag her large suitcase around with her. She crawled beneath the stiff, bleached sheets of the bed; the mattress showed serious signs of structural failure somewhere in the center. Laura positioned herself on her back so her buttocks rested in the indentation in the mattress. She closed her eyes and imagined herself back on the beach in the Virgin Islands on her honeymoon. She would lay her towel down on the sand and then wiggle her butt to make a perfect indentation in the sand that hugged the curves of her body. She reminisced fondly about the first time she ever saw the beach. It was so vast and powerful that it took her breath away. She had not seen a beach until her honeymoon with Jim, and the first sight of it made each one of her five senses cry out with exhilaration. She let herself remember the sound of the waves crashing and rolling on the shore, the sound of the birds calling as they flew into the air currents, seeming to stand still against the ocean breezes, floating like kites without strings. She could taste the salt in the air as she licked her lips and smelled the salty ocean air mixed with the fragrance of the tropical flowers that dotted the shoreline. She could feel the hot sand biting at her feet, granules creeping between each of her toes. And most of all, she could see the majestic power of the ocean, its deep color reaching out and wrapping around the horizon. Its immenseness astonished her, and she sensed its vibrant power, a power that had been in existence since before man walked the earth and that harbored more forms of life than ever walked the land.

Also in this vivid memory, she saw Jim standing beside her, holding her hand, seeing through her eyes as she absorbed the wonderful sight for the first time. He was responsible for exposing her to this beauty. She sat up in bed. She thought about digging in her purse for her cell phone and begging him to let her come home. She wanted to lie by his side and dream about the places he would take her, the sights she would never be able to see without him. She reached the table beside the bed and fumbled in her purse for the phone. She found it and pulled it into her lap. Laura sat there, the key pad lit up, inviting her to dial his number, until it finally went dark. She needed to evaluate her feelings before she made that call. Did she really love Jim or just his ability to take her places and buy her things? At first she did not mind how controlling and domineering he was; it was actually nice to have someone else make the decisions about her life. However, when Jim made the decision for her that she could not have children, her perspective changed. It was at that point she realized that the power he held over her might not be worth the price of admission to see all the places she had dreamed about. She didn't know the answer to these questions just yet. Maybe she needed time, like Jim suggested, to sort through her thoughts. Maybe Jim would begin to miss her as well and she could eventually change his mind and talk him into letting her have a baby.

Wrestling with these thoughts, she placed the phone in her purse and nestled back into her position in the indentation of the bed. Once again, she closed her eyes, only this time she didn't picture the beach. Her thoughts turned in another direction. She fell asleep dreaming of her days with Alex and the joy he brought her. She slept deeply and restfully.

Laura woke with the dawning of the day and decided not to shower in the small, moldy-smelling bathroom. She dressed and was packed by 7:00 a.m. Once again, she woke the clerk from his cot, wondering if she were the only guest staying at the motel. She returned her key and asked the man if there was any place to get breakfast in the area. She wanted to inquire further about the town she was trying to find, as well as sit down for the first time in days and eat a healthy breakfast. The man was equally as unhelpful as the night before. Laura got the impression that man might have information but was too eager to get back to bed to be bothered giving directions.

She returned to her lone car in the gravel parking strip and pulled back onto the winding two-lane road that snaked its way farther into the mountains. Now that it was daylight, Laura could see the spectacular view she had missed traveling the night before. The higher she climbed into the mountains, the smaller and less dense the trees became. Down in the valley, a deep green blanket of trees covered the horizon as far as her eyes could see. Smaller mountains and foothills rose and fell in gentle swells, giving variety and texture to the landscape. She realized that having grown up at this height, she had failed to realize the awesomeness of the environment around her. It was not until she returned that she appreciated the views that she took for granted as a child. She surmised this was probably similar to a child growing up living next to the ocean. That person would likely fail to realize the beauty of living on the ocean until he or she got out in the world, saw new places, and then returned home.

A blinking dashboard light interrupted Laura's thoughts. She realized she was low on gas. She looked at the map on her GPS, which indicated that a small town was just a few miles ahead, up the steeply inclining road. She hoped there was a gas station there; she had no idea what she would do if she ran out of fuel up here in the mountains. She watched in sick anticipation as the fuel gauge seemed to inch its way down with maddening speed as the car engine labored to climb the steep grade. A few miles before the town, she willed her car to make the climb on the precious remaining fuel. Finally, she saw buildings ahead and a familiar gas sign cocked lazily to one side of the sign post. Sure that the car was running on fumes, she pulled beside one of the two pumps and hoped that the station was open. She turned off the engine. There was a small store in the station, and she decided to get a map of the area. It might offer more details of the small towns; the GPS was increasingly unreliable the farther she got into the mountains. All technology was pretty useless in these undeveloped and satellite-unfriendly parts.

A man in coveralls approached her car, eyeing the shiny black BMW with interest.

"Hi. Can I get some gas? I am also interested in buying a map. Do you have any for sale?"

The man didn't respond right away. Then he nodded and held his hand out to her, indicating he needed money before he began fueling her car. She reached in her purse and handed him a credit card. He promptly handed it back and spoke one word.

"Cash."

Laura dug in her wallet and pulled out a fifty-dollar bill. The man took it and began filling her car. She stuck her head out the window and inquired again about the map.

"Can I buy a map?" she asked hopefully.

The man reached into his pocket with agonizing slowness and produced a set of keys. Laura opened her car door and followed him to the small store. Laura waited impatiently as the man tried each of a dozen keys in the lock before finding the right one. He retried certain keys more than once, and Laura had to fight the urge to rip them out of his hands and find the right one.

Ten agonizing minutes later, as she exited the store with a map, she saw people across the street entering a small deli-type restaurant nestled into the hillside, a rickety porch protruding from the front. Another car had parked alongside hers while she had been buying the map and was waiting patiently for its turn at the gas pump. Laura waited for the man in the overalls to top the fuel off at an even fifty dollars and replace the gas cap without hurry. She didn't wait for a receipt and pulled out of the station, looking for a spot across the street near the deli to park. She found a spot between two beefed-up pickup trucks with mud flaps and large tires, sporting gun racks in the back windows. Her shiny black car seemed out of place between the two muddy trucks. She left it hesitantly and walked into the deli, which had a sign out front that read, WE SERVE BREAKFAST LUNCH AND DINNER.

Laura seated herself at the counter and noticed two men in hunting clothes, including bright orange vests, sitting in a booth in the corner. They spoke in whispered tones and paused to stare at her a moment before resuming their hushed conversation. The stools were well-worn, and the cracked red linoleum counter was in serious need of makeover. The wooden boards under her feet were uneven; she had to pull her stool to a new position after she sat down in order to balance the legs. A few minutes later, a large woman with a waddling gate and a red checkered apron tied around her waist made her way to Laura with a menu in hand. Laura had spread her map out before her and was debating whether or not to ask the waitress if she had ever heard of Rimrock. Laura took the menu without speaking to the waitress, who had handed it to her and immediately walked over to chat with the two men in the booth. She opened the menu and decided against the scrapple and grits, two staples she had grown up eating but had no interest in eating again for nostalgia's sake. She chose a single egg over easy with bacon and wheat toast.

Five minutes later, the woman appeared with a pot of coffee. After pouring refills for the two men, she came to take Laura's order. Speaking in a familiar thick mountain dialect, the woman took Laura's order and poured her a cup of thick, black coffee. Laura politely asked for some cream and sugar, and the woman disappeared for another five minutes before returning with a small tray that held a spoon, cream, and sugar. Laura had a strong desire to drink her coffee and leave, but the smells wafting from the kitchen persuaded her to stay and eat her breakfast. She had no desire to talk to the waitress and ask her about Rimrock, so she studied the map, noticing the names and locations of towns that seemed to have a familiar ring from her past. She pinpointed the route she hoped would take her into her hometown, and then her breakfast arrived. It was fresh, hot, delicious, and well worth the wait.

# *Chapter 11*

LAURA FELT SATISFIED AND REENERGIZED when she pulled her car, still wedged between the two giant trucks, out of the small parking strip and found herself back on a windy upgrade. As quickly as the town appeared, it now disappeared behind her after the first bend in the road.

Having decided on the route to take, Laura felt sure she could find Rimrock. The town was not located on any major routes, and the small side roads she needed to take were not denoted on any map. However, her memories of the larger surrounding towns were enough to head her in the right direction. According to her calculations, she figured she could be in her hometown within the hour. The dangerous road curves and the poor conditions forced her to drive slowly, but she finally arrived at the last town on the map before she would begin to search for Rimrock.

The small town of Andes had grown considerably since the last time she was there. She could remember being taken there by her parents on special occasions, like shopping trips at Christmas and birthdays. Once in a blue moon they would come into Andes and watch a movie at the theater, but that was rare, since they lived in poverty and didn't have the money.

The town had built a small ski slope along the mountain above that included two chairlifts and two rope tows. The small mountain was not a big tourist attraction because of its size, but people who were not serious skiers and who just wanted to give the sport a try found it adequate for their needs. Laura was surprised to see a new summer attraction being advertised on a big billboard as she drove into the town: COME AND EXPERIENCE THE THRILL OF THE ALPINE SLIDE, LOCATED AT ANDES SKI SLOPE AND LODGE.

Besides the ski slope, the town's center featured a ski shop and restaurant, several quaint little gift shops, a gas station, a small grocery store, and a real-estate agency. Several of these businesses had been upgraded or remodeled since she had last been there, but basically everything looked the same. There was one major addition to the town, a Swiss chalet–looking motel that offered discounts on tickets to the ski slope to lodgers. Even though Laura had cringed every time she had to sit in the truck next to her father, she remembered the thrill of riding in her dad's pickup truck into Andes and dreaming what it would be like to live there.

As she drove slowly through the town, she spotted an establishment that held less-than-fond memories. Tucked back away from the road, a large dirt parking lot in front, was Bud's Tavern. Fourteen years later, the shabby building looked almost the same, except a few sections of the siding hung in disrepair, and she noticed a few shingles were missing from the roof. She had been around twelve when her dad forced her to go into the bar with him. Her mother had sent them into town to buy some groceries. Most of the time, Dad went by himself. Usually he did not return with groceries because he spent the money on alcohol at the bar. Knowing this was the case, Mother had sent Laura with him, desperately hoping that her presence would deter him from going to the bar. Unfortunately, she was dead wrong.

In an almost-unconscious act, Laura pulled her car to the side of the road across the street from the tavern and stared at it. She wished she had a match and the nerve to walk across the street and burn the place to the ground, erasing it from the earth and thus from her memory. She remembered the night her father dragged her out of the pickup and forced her to enter the bar with him. She had pleaded to stay in the truck, but it was winter and he told her she would freeze to death if she stayed in the truck. The moment they entered the bar, the thick smoke burned her eyes, and the smell of stale beer was overpowering. There were no women in the bar, only rugged mountain men. She could remember them all staring at her as her father dragged her across the dimly lit, smoke-filled room to the bar. Remembering that awful night, her heart pounded in her chest, and she began to shake as she recalled the fear that overtook her that evening.

Her dad started ordering beers, and she huddled under the bar at his feet, trying to make herself invisible. She shut her eyes and pretended that she was a bird, flying away, soaring into the sky away from that place.

Suddenly, a scruffy face appeared and stared at her in her inadequate hiding place.

"So, Joe, what do we have here?" the face said as it pressed close to hers, spewing spittle and beer-soaked breath at her.

"Laura, come on out here, darling, and let these men have a look-see," her father commanded.

Laura cringed and tried to melt into the base of the bar. Her father grabbed her by the forearm and pulled her out from under the bar. Her head crashed against the underside of the bar, and she saw stars for a moment.

"Well, let me see this perty little thang," the drunken man shouted. He pulled Laura over to him and sat her forcibly on his lap. Laura's head throbbed, and tears welled in her eyes.

A voice yelled across the room. "Ask her what she wants for Christmas, Jake. I bet you have sumthin' special to give her."

Bursts of laughter broke out across the room, and before she knew it, she was being flung from one drunken slob to another, each sitting her on their lap and fondling her, the stench of their breath and their bodies making her want to vomit. Finally, she couldn't stand it anymore. She screamed at her father to make them stop and to take her home. The tears ran down her cheeks, and her body shook with fright.

"All right now, boys, I guess I better get the brat home," he yelled over his shoulder, still absorbed in drinking his beer. Taking his time to finish the beer he had paid for, her father finally drained the last drops of the cherished liquid and collected his daughter, who was still being passed around the room like a rag doll. By this time, Laura's clothes were torn, and she was sobbing and shaking uncontrollably. He picked up her coat, which the drunken men had torn off of her, from the floor and led her out to the truck. Outside, her father threw her coat at her, but it was soaked with beer, so she dragged it along behind her, choosing to deal with the cold rather than the stench of beer. She could still remember some of the promises the men had whispered in her ear as they passed her around the room, and memories of what they wanted to do her made her shake with anger as she sat in the BMW.

Laura didn't remember the ride home or her mother coming to lead her out of the truck, screaming at her father, repeatedly asking what he had done to her. Laura remained in shock for a couple of days and then slowly, through sheer determination not to let her father destroy her, came back to the land of the living. She awakened feeling stiff and dirty, dried blood crusting her scalp where she had hit her head. Her mother had tried to give her a sponge bath, but her father kept screaming at her to leave her alone. He insisted that Laura was just trying to get out of doing her chores and that she'd better snap out of it or he'd give her a reason to hole up like a sick rabbit.

Laura rose and, despite the pain in her head, washed herself and returned to her routine existence. The coat she'd worn that night she never wore again. Even though her mother washed it, she could never bear to put it on due to the unpleasant memories it brought back.

Lost in the details of that horrible experience, Laura finally realized she had been sitting in a daze by the side of the road. Shaking the terrible memories from her mind, she reminded herself that all those events were in the past. Her father was dead, as likely were all the men in the bar that night, their livers equally pickled by the constant flow of alcohol they consumed.

She took the car out of park and drove out of town, searching her memory bank for some sign of recognition that would lead her back to Rimrock. Reaching the end of town, Laura came to an intersection that brought back a memory. A secondary road parted from the main road and rose steeply up an incline. While there was no name on the road, Laura could remember the grinding of gears her father's truck made when they made this first turn out of town. She distinctly remembered hoping that the truck would break down trying to climb the hill so they could go back into town and spend more time there.

Her BMW drove smoothly and powered up the incline. Soon the road leveled out and continued to wind its way toward a higher elevation. A few miles later, through a few more intersections, Laura arrived at a valley nestled between the peaks of two mountains. Laura began to perspire, even though the temperature in the car remained cool. A single ridge of rock protruded from one of the mountainside, and Laura knew when she saw the familiar sight that she was near the town named after the spectacular natural rock formation. A row of shacks appeared on her left, vacant and decaying. She'd known one of the families that lived in those shacks, and she wondered what had become of them. The only establishments that comprised the town of Rimrock came into view at the only intersection.

Laura remembered the small corner store that carried a limited stock of grocery items and some bait and tackle supplies and also served as a butcher shop for dressing deer and other game. It also dispensed hunting licenses, which were only purchased by out-of-towners. The only other stores consisted of a gas station/repair shop and a greasy-spoon diner. As Laura approached, she realized that all but the gas station were no longer in business. The other stores were boarded up and had long since closed their doors to the Rimrock customers who frequented them and socialized on their doorsteps most Saturday nights during summer.

Laura remembered meeting her first boyfriend on the steps of the diner. She was fourteen and had snuck out of her house to ride her bike into town. While she was afraid someone might see her and report back to her father, the sheer thrill of disobeying her father and the freedom she felt as she rode up to that diner outweighed the fear of being caught. She did eventually get caught a few times sneaking out, but through experience, she learned only to go out on a nights when her father passed out from drinking, minimizing the chances of detection. Her mother knew she was gone but never said a word to Laura.

Laura stopped her car at the intersection. The home she had known was off to the right, nothing more than a burned-out shell. Now that she was back in town, she could close her eyes and remember every bend and turn in the road that would lead her to the remains of the shack. She chose not to revisit the site.

The left branch of the intersection was the road that led to her aunt's house. Knowing the chances were slim that her aunt still lived there, she turned the corner and hoped for the best. At this point in her life, she had nowhere else to go and no one she could turn to for help. Finding her aunt was her only alternative. If that didn't pan out, she was going to have to come up with a new game plan. For now, it gave her a purpose and a mission. It was easy for her to remember the route to her aunt's house. Going there as a child was always a special treat. It meant she and her parents would dress up in clean clothes, and her father would usually treat her in a civilized manner, if only as an illusion for Aunt Gracie. Visiting meant an evening when she got to feast on sweet potatoes and desserts and some meat besides the venison or pork that her father raised. It was the only time in her childhood that she remembered being treated with respect, as part of the family instead of the burden that her father always accused her of being. They didn't get to go to her aunt's house nearly enough in Laura's eyes, only on holidays. Since her home did not have a telephone, those visits were the only time she had to get to know her aunt. She was so afraid of doing something to cause trouble and make the family have to go home that she usually spent the evenings as quiet as a mouse, as unobtrusive as possible. She only spoke when asked questions, and she remained on constant guard to use her best manners. Every visit, no matter what the occasion, her aunt would pull her into the kitchen through the swinging doors and fill her pockets with homemade cookies wrapped in napkins. She also always had a book or two to give Laura; reading was one of her only means of escaping and learning about the world around her. Books were her only real possessions, and she feasted on every one that her aunt kindly gave her.

As Laura picked her route through the mountainside, she noticed a lot of the familiar dwellings that dotted the route were no longer inhabited. Her hopes began to dwindle as she saw more and more deserted homes crumbling back to the earth from which they were built. She wondered why anyone would want to live here, now that there was nothing left in the area but a gas station—not that there was much to live for in this town in past years, but at least there had been some sense of community. Now a family would have to travel twenty miles back to Andes just to buy groceries.

Finally, her search was over. After fourteen years, Laura had located her hometown, driven through its sparse remains, and found the house that had been occupied by her only living relative. She had such mixed emotions about being there. She felt terrible guilt that she had run away after the fire, not even trying to contact her aunt. She'd been terribly afraid that she would be linked to the cause of the fire and put in jail for life for killing her father. Lighting that fire was self-defense in a way, but being young and naive, all Laura could think about was being alone in the world and having to face the justice system. Besides, what proof did she have that her father was an abusive monster? Would anyone believe her? Now, all she wanted to do was rekindle the relationship; her aunt was the only link left to the mother Laura had so desperately loved. Her greatest fear was that somehow word would get out that she was back and someone would start asking questions about where she had been, why she had left, and what really happened the night of the fire that killed her father. The fact that she was still plagued with nightmares about her past, especially the night of the fire, was proof that she hadn't experienced closure about that night. There had been no healing of her wounds and no resolution to her running away. Perhaps this visit was a needed step in dealing with her past. She made the decision to stop at the house and see if her aunt was still alive.

Laura peered up the driveway, toward the house, but saw no signs of life. An old Carolina blue Pontiac was parked in the driveway. The log home stood, sturdy as ever, its rustic exterior cleanly maintained and outlined by a row of bushes and flowers. The driveway inclined slightly, and Laura's tires spun on the rocks momentarily before catching to proceed up the single-lane drive. Laura was terrified that after she found the nerve to knock on the door, the door would open and the face answering it would not be her aunt's but a complete stranger's. Even though she was terrified, she knew she had to finish what she started and complete her quest.

She turned off the engine and sat for a second, collecting her thoughts and gaining the nerve to get out of the car and knock on the door. If her aunt didn't answer the door, she wanted to be able to explain coherently what she was doing and why she was invading their privacy. If her aunt did answer the door, she wanted to say just the right things to make her aunt understand why she was there.

Taking a deep breath, Laura opened the door and then closed it behind her, feeling the butterflies dance in her stomach as they hadn't done in years. She climbed the front steps, walked to the door, and took hold of the brass knocker. She struck the brass ring against the plate in a series of quick raps and waited for a response. A minute passed. Laura was tempted to retreat. She could just get back in the car, drive away, and spend a quiet week back at the Swiss Chalet in Andes and do her thinking. *No*, she told herself, *keep trying*. It would be foolish to turn away before she'd positively determined if her aunt still lived there. Resolutely, she grabbed the knocker and rapped again several times, this time louder. Her efforts were rewarded with a soft shuffling from inside the house. The knob turned, and the heavy door swung open.

The thin-framed woman, appearing to be in her early seventies, wore a gray dress, a colorful floral apron tied around her waist. Her gray hair was piled neatly on her head in a bun. Her bright eyes twinkled, and a touch of surprise could be heard in her voice as she stared at Laura and asked, "May I help you, young lady?"

Laura stood as still as a statue, unable to speak for a second. "Aunt Gracie? Is that you? It's me, Laura, your niece."

The older women stared at Laura in disbelief, like Laura was a spectral presence that suddenly appeared before her very eyes.

"Oh, Lord have mercy. Laura, where have you been all these years, child?"

Her aunt swept Laura into her arms. Laura nestled herself into her aunt's bosom as she cried uncontrollably into her shoulder. She smiled between her tears, realizing that her aunt still smelled like fresh-baked cookies.

The two women embraced fiercely, trying to shrink all the years that had separated them. Each one cried soft words to the other, repeating how they had missed one another and how it was a miracle they were together once again. All the while, Laura was wondering how she could have blocked the memory of how much she loved this woman from her mind all those years. Maybe, she thought, she had blocked all the details from her childhood to help erase the pain of leaving behind everything and everyone she ever knew. It would have been too painful to keep in touch with her aunt because her aunt was a connection to the pain she was running from. It felt so right to be here now, and she knew now that she had made the right decision in coming here and reconnecting with her beloved aunt. There was much healing to be done, and part of that was going to be facing her past. That could only be accomplished with someone's help and by someone who understood and knew what she had been through.

Both women needed tissues to blow their noses and wipe their teary eyes, and Aunt Gracie led Laura into her home and closed the heavy door behind them.

# Chapter 12

As Laura regained her composure, she glanced around the living room she had so loved as a child. The same familiar handmade quilts decorated the same worn but well-cared-for furniture. The air smelled the same, like furniture polish and laundry soap and a delicate musty odor, all rolled into one. A large handmade oval braided wool rug lay on the hardwood floor in front of the fireplace. Laura could remember the story of how the sisters, her mother and her aunt, had spent long hours by the fire braiding and sewing the rug one long, cold winter.

Her aunt, she noticed had grown shorter with age. Laura could remember her being a lot taller. She wasn't sure if she had really shrunk that much or if she seemed taller because Laura had been so young when she last saw her. Her hair, showing flecks of gray in Laura's last memory, was transformed into a uniform grayish white, remaining full and lustrous for a woman of her age. The skin on her face was a bit more wrinkled, and the skin on her hands had begun to take on the transparent, mottled look of an aging person. Otherwise, her aunt appeared to be as healthy and vibrant as the last time Laura saw her.

Laura needed to use the bathroom, and as she excused herself she passed a handmade doll with a crocheted dress and a porcelain face. Laura stopped and looked back at her aunt. As a child, the first thing she would do when she entered her house was to run and check under the doll's dress. When she lifted the hem, there was always a piece of hard candy waiting for her, as if by magic. Laura smiled at the memory, and Aunt Gracie smiled back and nodded. Laura gently lifted the hem, and there was the magical piece of hard candy waiting for her, as if her aunt knew she would return at any moment and check for it. Laura's eyes teared up again, and she took the delicious candy and placed it in her mouth. She couldn't remember the name of the candy, but it came in little tins and was shaped like fruit. She also couldn't remember a more savored taste in her entire life.

In the bathroom, Laura washed her face with cold water and tried to calm the storm of emotions flowing through her mind. She needed to collect herself so she could sit down and recount the years of life that had passed to her aunt. She knew that many of the memories she was about to dredge up were going to be unpleasant ones that needed to be expunged from her mind. She dried her face with the hand towel and returned to find her aunt had already started the water boiling for tea and had brought out a plate of cookies. The two sat down on the couch and made idle conversation until the teapot whistled from the kitchen. Aunt Gracie disappeared through the swinging doors and returned with two steaming cups of tea.

When the proper amount of sugar and milk were added to the tea, and Laura had eaten a few of the cookies, Gracie took Laura's hands in her own and looked her directly in the eyes.

"It is time, child," she told Laura. "It is time to tell me everythin' that has happened to you. I want to know everythin', from the time you ran away from this place to the time you drove back to my door. I've spend fourteen years waitin' for the day you would come back, afraid to leave or move in case you couldn't find me."

Laura felt shattered by that statement. "Aunt Gracie, you spent all these years here waiting for me to come back?"

"Yes, child. Everyone needs a place to come home to. I'm the only one left you could return to. I knew it was just a matter of time. Everyone told me you were dead, that you burned in that fire, but I knew in my heart that you were still alive."

Laura hugged her aunt, refusing to let her tears flow again. Laura released her aunt and took a sip of the warm, sweet tea. Taking a deep breath, she recounted her journey from the time she left home at sixteen to the present day. She omitted the details of how the cabin caught on fire, not ready to confess to murdering her father. She began with seeing the flames light up the house and running in fear for her own life—running in fear and not turning back. She apologized for not coming to see her aunt, wanting to get as far away from her former life as possible so as not be found by her father. She recounted how she went to a friend's house and borrowed some clothes and a few dollars so she could hitchhike down the mountain to the city of Boone. She made her friend swear an oath to never tell anyone she had been there. She told her aunt about each job she had worked at, trying to keep herself off the streets, and how she stayed in shelters while she saved enough money to finally rent her own place. She poured out her feelings of accomplishment when she landed the first job that wasn't waitressing or washing dishes, an actual job with a desk and a salary. It was her first taste of being self-sufficient, of having no one to answer to, able to make her own decisions. She recounted her long hours of dedication to the office she worked at without promotion so she could buy furniture for her little apartment and join a gym. And finally, she talked about meeting Jim, her husband. She told the facts of their meeting and engagement and the year of marriage and how she felt like she had been swept away in some fairy tale until just a week ago. The events of the past week had made her think long and hard about what she wanted out of life and who she was.

Her aunt sat quietly, not interrupting to ask questions or to comment, just listening and nodding occasionally. When Laura concluded her tale, she noticed that it had grown dark outside. The hours had flown by in some kind of time warp. Her mouth was dry and her throat sore from talking so much. Again the two women hugged, and her aunt once again retreated to the kitchen, this time to prepare a meal for her niece. Laura wanted to get up and help, but she lay down on the couch, exhausted from the emotional baggage she had just unloaded. He aunt woke her from the light sleep she drifted into and encouraged her to eat some supper. Laura ate, and then her aunt guided her back to the couch and covered her with the handmade quilt that lay draped over the back. Laura slept better that night than she had since she could remember. It was the kind of sleep a person falls into after the mind has been cleansed and the heart has been healed, when a feeling of love surrounds you like a warm, downy quilt.

Morning arrived. Laura awoke to the smells of bacon and eggs and coffee. She stretched out from the curled position she had lain in all night, surprised to find she had not changed position even once during the night. It was a wonderful feeling to have someone cooking breakfast, providing that motherly care that Laura had missed for so many years. She rolled off the couch and found her shoes, which she didn't remember taking off the night before, and put them on so she could go out to the car and retrieve her suitcase. Back inside, lugging the heavy bag, she yelled into the kitchen that she would be taking a quick shower before breakfast. Her aunt yelled back that it better be quick because breakfast was almost ready.

Laura showered and was dried and dressed just as Gracie was setting the table for breakfast. While they ate, Gracie asked Laura a few of the questions she had carefully saved. She wanted to know what type of wedding she'd had, what the townhouse was like where she and Jim lived, and if she planned on going back to Tanner Mountain to look for Alex. The first few questions were easy to answer, but the last one took Laura by surprise.

"You don't think I still have a chance of finding him, do you, Aunt Gracie?" Laura asked hopefully.

"Well, dear, I told you everyone comes home sooner or later. Alex might be lookin' for you right now. I can tell that the bond you two had together is not gonna be broken by a separation. With all the thinkin' you have to do right now, I think it might be a healthy thing for you to go on off and spend a little time with nature. And while you're out there straightenin' things out in your mind, you might just run into Alex. "

Laura was astonished by the woman's wisdom. She seemed to know exactly the right things to say at any given moment.

"Why don't we pack you a couple of days' supplies? Take a little campin' trip back to where you were when Alex disappeared. Give it a day or two and then come on back here to me. At least you'll find peace in the notion that you tried to find him."

Laura felt excited by the idea. Her aunt knew that she was capable of camping alone because she had survived and succeeded in a situation that would have devastated most women. But her aunt had something more to say to her.

"I know it was your turn to talk yesterday and explain all that happened to you over the years. Now I have some apologizin' and explainin' of my own to do. I want to tell you why I never took you away from your father all those years ago, why I sat by and let all those bad things happen to you. You see, Laura, your momma was my sister. And as bad as your daddy was, I knew two things. One, that if I took you away, it would break your momma's heart. She lived only for you, you know. And secondly, I knew your daddy's sense of pride. If I had taken you away, he would have blamed your momma. I think he would have ended up killing her. I couldn't let that happen either. I was just sick inside, knowing these things and having to keep them all inside like a deep, dark secret. After the fire I grieved for your momma, and I figured you had run away. I was so scared for you, child. I wanted to find you and bring you here, but I didn't even know where to begin to look. I figured when the time was right, you would come back to me. And look, here you are."

Laura stood and hugged her aunt. "I know that you loved me. And I know that you were too kind to take me from Momma. Don't blame yourself. Everything worked out okay, except I wish that Momma had outlived Daddy so we could all have been together when I came back."

"If wishes were trees, then we would be surrounded by forests," Gracie replied. "We need to worry about the livin' right now, mainly you and me and Alex. We can decide what to do about your husband later. He doesn't sound like he's too worried about you, tellin' you to take some time off and come back later."

"He was just trying to work things out the only way he knows how," Laura said, not sure why she felt the need to defend Jim.

Gracie cleared the breakfast dishes and then proceeded to pack Laura food for a couple of days on Tanner Mountain. While Gracie packed, Laura got her map from her car and planned the route she would take to get there. Her aunt made her promise not to be gone longer than three days. She said if she didn't hear from her by then, she was going to send the Rangers in after her. Gracie had an old sleeping bag stored in her garage that Laura could take on her trip. She found a tarp and a piece of rope she could use to make a lean-to. She wouldn't be as well-equipped as she and Jim were on the first trip, but she was looking forward to the challenge.

Laura hated leaving her aunt again so soon after finding her, but she knew that this was just a stopping point she needed in order to regroup and make a game plan for her future. Her aunt had lived alone too long to have Laura stay there permanently, and Laura couldn't survive living near Rimrock again. While her aunt's home was a safe harbor, there were too many bad memories in the area for Laura to ever live there happily again.

Her aunt accompanied her to the car and asked to sit in the shiny black BMW, just to get a feel.

"You know, I've seen cars like this now and again in town. I always wondered what they were like inside. I never dreamed you'd be pullin' up in my driveway in one of these fancy new cars."

"Climb in, Aunt Gracie, and let me show you some of the things this car can do. Do you know you can make the seats warm in the winter?"

Gracie gasped in surprise as Laura eased her into the rich leather seat on the driver's side. She had never seen a car with so many gadgets. She played with the electric seat warmer, individualized temperature controls, and electric seat adjustments, like a little kid. When her curiosity had been satisfied, Laura helped her out of the car and gave her a good-bye hug and kiss. Laura still couldn't help feeling a sense of regret over parting so soon from her aunt. Gracie felt the same, she could sense it, but she also knew Gracie was trying to do the right thing and send her off to where she could make her own decisions and think clearly without being swayed by someone else's opinion. Just one day after finding her long-lost aunt, Laura pulled back out of the driveway and headed back to Tanner Mountain on her next adventure.

# Chapter 13

THE DRIVE TO TANNER MOUNTAIN brought back all the unpleasant memories that Laura had experienced during and after that first trip. The only bright spot had been meeting her new friend the veterinarian and the experience of being able to help each other at a point in their lives when they both needed it. She wondered if she still had his card, and she reached in her purse and pulled out her wallet. Sure enough, his business card was tucked safely away in the card section. She made a mental note to locate the town he lived in on the map, so if she ever passed through, she might find the nerve to look him up.

Concentrating on her driving, Laura worked on her game plan for camping on the mountain. The first night she planned to stay in the same place she and Jim had stayed. Then a frightening thought occurred. Those men that she and Jim had encountered—what if they found her and realized that she was alone? They had been civil only because the land had not been taken from them yet. What if the land deal had gone through by now and they were hostile, trying to protect themselves from people coming in and developing their land? They were likely to shoot at anyone they saw, thinking it might be the developer's crew.

Laura wondered if camping alone there was a good idea, but then she thought about Alex. Perhaps she would camp in a different location and revisit the old campsite during the day, when she could keep a lookout for the men. Confident that her skills in the forest were enough to keep her hidden if she didn't want to be seen, she felt sure she could protect herself as long as she stayed alert to the possible dangers.

The road narrowed to a two-lane road, and Laura found the dirt road that Jim had first taken her up. She noticed fresh tire tracks as she drove slowly up the road, avoiding the deepest potholes. When she came to the end, she was surprised to see two utility vehicles parked beside one another. The thought crossed her mind that these trucks were linked to Jim's company, but it was too late to turn back now. Laura didn't feel safe leaving her car for whoever was here to see, so she looked around for possible places to hide her vehicle. Back down the road fifty feet or so, she remembered passing a trail that looked wide enough to accommodate a car. She backed down the road until she found the trail entrance again. It was apparently an old logging road that at one time Rangers probably used to drive to a tower or some forest-based Ranger station. Taking her chances, Laura drove carefully onto the overgrown tracks and pulled her car forward until she felt it was hidden from view from the road. Someone passing by quickly would probably not notice a car had recently turned down the road, but she was sure it would be detected if anyone was seriously looking for her.

She gathered her supplies and strapped on the backpack her aunt had provided, and she walked back up the road toward the two vehicles. She found the trail that started up toward the rocky outcropping where she and Jim had originally camped. Signs that people had been through the area were prevalent: footprints, broken branches, and even cigarette butts. Laura kept her ears and eyes open as she followed the obvious trail through the woods. In two hours, she arrived within a hundred feet of where she and Jim had first camped. She was so preoccupied with determining where the people from the two vehicles might be that she didn't take time out to look for Alex. Sure enough, in the clearing above the outcropping of rocks, she heard men's voiced engaged in conversation.

Laura sank to her hands and knees and crawled to a grouping of pine trees that was dense enough to provide cover while still allowing her to hear the men's conversation. As far as she could tell, there were four or five of them, and they seemed to be heatedly discussing something. Crawling as close as she dared, she listened hard but still could not make out what there were saying. Twenty yards ahead, she noticed a boulder. If she could get there undetected, it would give her protection while allowing her to clearly hear the men. As far as she knew, these people were no threat to her, so even if she was detected she would probably be safe. She decided to take her chances. Staying as low to the ground as possible, she crept as silently as a cat through the tall grass and then crouched behind the boulder, less than fifteen feet from the men. From this vantage point, she could clearly hear the conversation.

"We got the location; we just have to decide the best way to get there from here," she heard one man say.

"I still don't understand why Tom and Jim can't go do their own dirty work. Why should we be risking our necks for this backstabbing company?" another voiced answered in disgust.

The hairs on the back of Laura's neck stood up at the mention of Tom and Jim's names and the mention of doing "dirty work."

"Look, Einstein, it doesn't take a rocket scientist to figure out that if we don't do this little task for them, then we are going to end up like the others who tried to question their motives—jobless. Either we join 'em and share in the profits or leave and keep our mouths shut. Since we are already here, I suggest we get this over with and get out of here before we get caught."

Laura disliked the situation less as time passed. She thought about her aunt and some of the other good people she knew from her past who lived in the mountains, and she pictured them as the victims. That thought made her burn with anger. She became determined not to run away from the situation, as her better judgment suggested she should. She remained as the men debated some more about which route would be best to cross the top of the mountain and find the location of the house they were looking for. Half the group wanted to go directly over the top. The other half wanted to go around the side and avoid the steep inclines.

The vote for over the top won, and the group started climbing directly up the slope behind them. Laura slid around to the other side of the boulder so her body was still hidden from their view as the men changed position. She sat still and tried to decide what to do next. She know the men were going to threaten the people who owned the property—of that she was sure. If she left and went to get help, there was no way she could be sure that help would arrive in time, not to mention she didn't know where to send the help. If she got involved herself, then she could be in danger. She doubted if any men in the company would actually hurt her because she was Jim's wife. There could be other consequences, though, that would not be pleasant.

Trying not to think of the consequences, Laura took off her backpack and tucked it under the ledge of the boulder she was hiding behind. She could not follow in stealth mode with the huge pack on her back. After the pack was hidden as well as possible, Laura started trailing the men up the mountain. Mountain men they were not, and they proceeded slowly and noisily up the slope. Suddenly, Laura had a brainstorm. It was a risky plan. If she were called on her bluff, then she could be placing herself in grave danger, but she decided it was worth a try. Jumping up from her crouched position, she sprinted easily into yelling distance of the men. This plan of action was based on two very important variables. One, that these men did not know Laura and Jim had split up, and two, they were dumber than they looked.

Laura shouted to the group of men on the slope above her. "Hey, ya'll, come down here. I have an important message from Jim and Tom."

The men stopped in their tracks and looked at each other with mild suspicion. They turned and stared back down the slope toward Laura. Laura was using all her survival skills to remain as calm and poker-faced as possible. One of the men approached her; she breathed heavily, as if she had been running.

"I'm so glad I caught up to you. Jim sent me after you because, well, I am from these parts originally, you know, and he knew I was in the best shape of anyone in the office."

She breathed heavily, using her most disarming smile and trying not to appear nervous.

"Well, what's the message?" one of the men asked with curiosity.

"The message is that you are not to go through with your plans," she said thoughtfully, trying to sound as if she had memorized the message. "Jim says to tell you that they found another way to force the people to sell."

"You are telling me that we came all this way for nothing? I thought they had run out of options, and that is the whole reason we are here," the man stated, seeming rather confused.

"I'm just relaying the message I was told to bring. You do whatever you have to now, but consider the message delivered. "

"You better be damn sure you got it right, because if those papers don't get signed by tomorrow, the company is going to lose this property to the state. I wouldn't want to be the one to mess up this deal, lady."

The men stood looking at one another. Some looked relieved; others looked agitated. Laura turned, as if satisfied she had completed her mission, and began to jog back down the hill.

"Hold it right there, Laura," a voice yelled down after her.

Laura froze at the sound of her name and the tone of the man's voice. A man she recognized from the office stepped forward. He was one of the men who stared at her when she walked down the hallway to visit Jim. She had also met him at some of the office functions. She didn't think he was friends with Jim. But perhaps she was wrong and Jim had confided in him that the two of them had separated.

"I haven't seen you near the office in a while. Jim said you were on a vacation or something."

Laura panicked for a moment and then regained her composure. She tried to mix a little truth into the scenario.

"I was away looking for my dog. Jim and I came up here last week so he could show me the site for the resort, and we lost him. I gave up and went home last night. I was out here all week," she said, trying to look sad.

"Yeah, that's right," another man chimed in. "Jim told me about the hillbilly brothers who threatened him with their hunting rifles when they were up here looking around."

Laura signed in relief. She had done it. She turned and continued back down the slope, eager to get as much distance as she could between her and the group of men. She was much quicker on her feet than they were and soon lost sight of them. She hoped they would return to their vehicles and go home for the night, not report back to the office. That would give Laura the night and part of the next day to look for Alex and get off the mountain before the goons could return and possibly harm her for foiling their plans. As for Jim, she would give anything to be a fly on the wall when the men reported that Laura tracked them down and gave them a message to discontinue their plan of action. Jim would be furious beyond belief. Served him right for the way he treated her, totally underestimating her intellect and resourcefulness. If Jim had taken the time to understand Laura and her past, nothing like this would have been a surprise. Right now, she wanted to get her pack and head in a new direction to look for Alex.

Laura climbed down to the base of the mountain and decided to make camp there. She was confident the men would not venture down the mountain; they were probably exhausted from their day's hiking. She hung her tarp over the rope stretched between two trees and then gathered some twigs to build a fire so she wouldn't have to search around in the dark. When everything was set up to her satisfaction, she headed off in a new direction around the base of the mountain, hoping to stumble across a den or some type of shelter that Alex might have adopted as his home. She only hoped that she didn't run across anything else, like another bear or a mountain lion that may have made its home at the base of the mountain.

Laura proceeded cautiously, searching without success for any signs of dog prints the size of Alex's. Disappointed and tired, she returned to her campsite as night closed in and the last of the sun's rays became cloaked by the mountain that loomed above her. She got her fire started before the night sky turned densely black. She warmed the can of Dinty Moore stew her aunt had provided and then sat back to watch the night unfold.

The moon was almost full, eventually rising from around the edge of the mountain and shining brightly down on Laura. She stared at the moon, trying to picture the face people imagined they saw in its ruddy surface. The stars displayed themselves in all their brilliance. The night sky was so clear she could even make out the band of the Milky Way, stretching its white stream across the black background. In a streaking flash across the edge of her field of vision, Laura saw a shooting star. She turned her head quickly enough to see it as it disappeared over the horizon, its bright tail flashing out with a wink.

Laura closed her eyes and made a wish. It had been so long since she had seen a shooting star that she almost forgot that seeing it meant she could make a wish. There were so many possibilities but only one logical choice, given the circumstances.

"I hope and pray that I find my dog, Alex," she said out loud.

She somehow felt that by uttering her wish out loud for the world to hear, it had a better chance of coming true. With that happy thought still on her mind, she crawled into her tarp shelter and tried to fall asleep. She had so much on her mind that sleep eluded her. She was really worried about Jim's reaction to her interference with his plan. She was concerned about the mountain men finding her while she slept and shooting her, although the reality of that was negligible. She also worried that the men from the office would come back and hurt her before she had a chance to finish her search and get off the mountain. She didn't have any idea what chain reaction she had set off with her intervention—what changes in the flow of the universe her impulsive decision had caused. She could feel the ripples forming in the path of her life, as if she had just thrown a big rock into a pond. She could see the ripples spreading and getting larger and larger.

Before she went to sleep, she prayed for a miracle. She prayed that she would find Alex in the morning and be long gone before the men returned. She prayed that Jim would forgive her and that there was some way things could be resolved between them. She really did want the fairy-tale life they had together, but with a loving and trustful relationship and some children. She knew this was asking a lot. Lastly, she gave thanks for finding her Aunt Gracie and for the happiness and peace the reunion had brought her. Then she drifted off to sleep, comforted by the sounds in the forest.

The rays of the sun shone across Laura's face and gently woke her from a sound sleep. The ground she had slept on was hard, but apparently her sleep had not suffered because of that. The warm sun and morning breeze had already erased the damp, dewy moisture from the forest. Laura brushed her teeth and rinsed her mouth with water from her canteen. She felt she didn't have time for breakfast. She grabbed a granola bar and devised a plan to search as much of the area as she could before noon and then return to her car and head back to Gracie's house. She figured that the car posed the greatest threat to her; that was the one location where she knew she could be trapped. No man working for the company could track her or keep up with her in the forest.

Packing her supplies in her pack, Laura again felt a sense of futility concerning her search for Alex. She knew in her heart that unless she found some sign of him, this would be the last attempt she would make to look for him. Trying not to depress herself with negative thoughts, Laura made a new plan to search toward the top of the mountain. Perhaps he had gone in the direction the local men had come from, hoping to find people.

She trudged back up the slope, drawing energy from the knowledge that she had a time frame to which she needed to adhere. When she'd climbed halfway back up the mountain, she found a small grassy meadow and sat down for a quick rest.

"Popular place, this mountain is of late," a man's voice said from behind her.

Without turning around Laura replied, "Well, I haven't been here once that I haven't run into somebody."

Then she turned around to face the person talking to her. Laura immediately recognized the younger of the two men she and Jim had encountered on their first trip. He was alone this time, without a gun. He had a more serious look on his face, not the sloppy grin of a man who had been sipping whiskey before breakfast. Laura didn't fear the man as she had during their first encounter, and for that she was thankful.

"I saw you here before, didn't I?" the man remarked.

Laura held out her hand in a friendly way and said, "Yes. My name is Laura. What's yours?"

The man looked unsure and eyed her with his head cocked to one side. Then, making some sort of decision, he extended his hand and said, "Pete."

"Nice to meet you, Pete. I want you to know right up front that I am not here with those men from the company. In fact, I risked my neck yesterday to help your family."

Pete listened with no change in expression.

"They wanted to come to your house and threaten you to make you sign the papers to buy your land, but I tricked them into leaving."

"Wasn't you the lady that lost the dog?" Pete suddenly interrupted.

"Yes!" Laura exclaimed. "Have you seen him?" she asked hopefully.

"Well, I reckon I saw somethin' that might have been him."

"What do you mean, might have been him?"

"Well, me and Buck was out huntin' the other day and we shot us a rabbit. The rabbit took a hit and kept runnin' for a while, but we done know that we would find him dead when he finally bled out. We caught up to him shore 'nough, but just as Buck took aim to finish him off, this gold streak came flyin' outta nowhere and carried the bastard off. Buck was bout to shoot after it, but I told him I thought that was the dog the man and lady was lookin' fur. Buck wanted to shoot him anyways cause he don't like nothin' carryin' off his game. He took a shot, but the dog was long gone with our rabbit."

Laura listened, not sure whether she was happy that Alex might have been spotted or horrified that people were shooting at him for stealing rabbits.

Coming to her senses, she asked, "Do you think you could take me to where you shot that rabbit? I'd really appreciate it. In fact, if you help me find him, I'll give you a reward … a hundred dollars," she added quickly, hoping she had that much cash with her.

Laura couldn't tell if the young man was happy or offended at the offer. He suddenly looked very distracted, as if he hadn't even heard what Laura had just asked him. He peered over Laura's shoulders and stared, unmoving, into the woods beyond her. He reminded her of the deer she had watched from her quiet hiding spots in the woods as a child. The deer would wander into the area totally relaxed, eating, moving about in the herd. Suddenly, one would raise its head, and the entire herd would imitate the first one and freeze. They would stand still, their ears cocked forward like radar dishes, their eyes glued to one important spot in the forest. They would all transform into statues. Then they would either return to grazing or bolt with leaps and bounds back into the forest.

Laura waited to see what the man would do. She half expected him to turn and bolt into the woods above the small clearing.

"Somebody's comin'," he said in a matter-of-fact tone.

Laura considered her senses sharper than the average person's, but even she could not detect any noises coming from the forest.

"Are you sure? I didn't hear a thing," she said, slightly worried.

"I gotta go. I gotta go tell Buck that they're back," Pete informed her. Then he turned and moved with amazing speed and agility back up the mountain. In seconds, he had disappeared from sight.

Laura wanted to turn and follow him and get him to take her to where he had last seen what he thought was her dog. On the other hand, she was afraid of whoever it was that the man heard coming.

Deciding to avoid an encounter if possible, Laura made her way back down the mountain the way she had come. She planned to circle around the men and arrive back on the trail behind them and then use her speed and superior conditioning to get back to her car long before they detected her. She was banking on the fact they hadn't discovered her car hidden down the road just below their own. She now wished that she had covered the car with some kind of brush and concealed the tracks from the dirt road.

Laura's speed and agility had been sharpened by her workouts and recent climbing, but being in shape had no impact on what happened next. In her hurry to descend around the edge of the grassy clearing and head back down the steep slope, she placed her foot on a small boulder in order to launch herself over it. Her foot slipped, jolting her forward. She tried to balance herself and prevent her momentum from carrying her dangerously down the slope. Unfortunately, the speed with which she was moving forward and downward was too great, and she lost her balance and tumbled anyway. She felt her ankle twist painfully sideways as she fell forward. Instead of thrusting her arms forward and taking the impact of her fall on her wrists, Laura tucked and rolled, landing on the soft padding of her backpack as she tumbled down the hillside. A sharp pain radiated from her ankle, which she knew was not a good sign. When she finally stopped rolling she assessed her condition. Besides being dirty and disheveled, various other parts of her body felt bruised, but she didn't think anything other than her ankle was injured.

The first thing she did was look up to see if she was in view of anyone who might be standing in the meadow. She didn't see anyone, so she started brushing herself off and testing weight on the ankle. Grabbing the branch of a tree for support, she placed all her weight on her good ankle and pulled herself to a standing position. Tenderly, she put weight on the damaged ankle, which had immediately started to throb when she moved. Stabbing pains, like hot knives, forced her to immediately remove weight from the ankle. A sick feeling began to rise in the pit of her stomach, and Laura whimpered and tried to hold back the tears that demanded to pour out. She felt like a child who had just lost an important game and was hurt in the process. She wanted to yell out, "Okay, you win. I quit. I want to go home now." She wanted to be comforted by her mother, settled on the couch with a quilt and an ice pack, and told that everything would be okay. She knew, however, that that was a fantasy and that she might have gotten herself in over her head this time.

Reality was a rude awakening. She had to think what to do and make good decisions. She couldn't let the pain interfere with her judgment. She had to alter the game plan but continue with the journey. She took a deep breath and visualized herself being strong and coping with the problem. She took off her backpack and searched through it until she found a rope and a bandana. With her camping knife, she cut a small portion of the rope. She found a thick branch from the pine tree above her on the ground and snapped off two even-length sticks from it. After fashioning a makeshift splint from the branches, rope, and bandana, Laura again tested her weight on her ankle. The pain was still great but less than it had been, and she thought she could walk if the terrain was not too steep. She found a stick nearby to use as a crutch. Of course, she now had only one option, to return to the car, which meant taking the same path as she feared the men would also be traveling.

Wearing her backpack again and trailing her walking stick, Laura dropped to her hands and knees and crept back up the slope to the clearing. Each time her foot accidentally bumped the ground, it sent shooting pains up her leg. Behind the clearing, voices emanated from the woods. She stood and limped across it to the nearest trees, just in time to hear the crackling footsteps and voices of at least two men. As their voices became clearer, she could hear their conversation.

"Even if we find her, what good is it going to do now?" one voice asked. Laura pressed herself against the back of the tree she was hiding behind, praying that she could not be seen from the clearing.

"When are you going to learn? We don't ask questions, we just follow instructions. Laura messed up the deal. The state of North Carolina got the property because we didn't force them to sign the contract with us. People are pissed, and somebody's got to pay. Would you rather it be us? Huh? I'm just happy that Tom and Jim are blaming her instead of us for being fools and listening to her."

"I want you to promise that we're just going to mess her up and convince her to get herself away to someplace safe. We could hang if anyone found out about this, you know. I don't want murder hanging on my head," the second man stated with concern.

"We're going to let her know that she has been a bad girl and that she doesn't mess around with the big boys. I guarantee that if she wasn't married to Jim she would be as lost as her little doggie and that nobody would ever find her again."

Laura held her breath as the men passed a few feet from her and stood looking around the clearing.

"Jim said she would be somewhere on this side of the mountain, not far from where they camped and lost the dog. Let's split up. You go up the mountain. I'll go down. If you find her, tell her we just want to talk and then bring her back here. We'll have some fun with her together. Got it?" the man in charge commanded.

"Yeah, I got it," the other replied tersely.

Laura waited until she felt sure both men had gone far enough not to hear her, and she slipped out from her hiding spot and limped as fast as she could down the trail. Pain from her ankle flared, but it was nothing compared to the flare of anger coming from her mind. This was the twenty-first century, and people did not go around messing up women for blowing business deals. This was not right. She shouldn't be running through the woods like a wounded animal, hiding from a couple of trained apes. She had half a mind to march back to the city and go to the police. She would provide a witness that the company was trying to use extortion to force the poor mountain people to sell their land and then tell them about the threats they just made against her. The problem was she had no proof. Who was going to believe her against an entire corporation of crooked men? At least she knew now why the people in the office were so unfriendly. They were working for crooks, and if they made a wrong move, they could be taking a long walk off a short pier.

Despite her pain, she was fueled by her growing anger along the gentle slope of the trail. She fed that anger and used it to keep her mind occupied and directed away from the pain. Another thought angered her even more. If it hadn't been for the goons showing up, she might be finding Alex right now. She felt sure the young man would have taken her to where he last saw him. The more she thought about their interference, the angrier she grew.

When she finally reached the trailhead and the area where her car was hidden, anger had clouded her judgment. Instead of taking precautions and approaching her car carefully, looking for signs that it had been discovered, she burst through the brush like an angry bull. Standing there, leaning against her car, was Jim. Her anger dissipated like a puff of smoke and instantly turned to fear as she recognized the look of anger on Jim's face.

"You just couldn't leave things along, could you?" The words seethed from Jim. She could tell that he had been standing there a long time, waiting to deliver this speech. He didn't even take notice of her torn clothing, the cuts on her face, or her bandaged ankle. It was as if he was oblivious to anything but her presence and focused only on his goal of vengeance. Laura froze and waited for the words that would rain like blows.

"We could have had it all. I could have been successful and climbed to the top. All you had to do was hitch a ride. You had it all in the palm of your hand, and you threw it away. We would have traveled and ventured to new and exciting places, and I would have bought you diamonds and beautiful clothes and made you a queen. That is why I picked you, you know. You were like a diamond in the rough. I wanted to chisel away your rough exterior and make you shine like a gem, make you something to love and cherish the rest of my life."

Jim had approached her, and she stood still, unsure of what to say, or what to do. She stood there, stunned, listening to him reveal his perfect plan for her life.

"We even had a chance to patch things up before this little incident. A little dissention can bring a couple closer, you know, but treason and betrayal—Laura, that is unacceptable. Did you know that Tom sent those men out to hurt you? I came out here to save your life. I knew you were too smart to get caught and that you would show up here. They all think I want to hurt you too. I had to let them think that, or I would be considered a traitor too. Now, Laura, you have screwed everything up, so there is only one option. Do you know what that is?"

He asked the question but didn't give her time to answer. Her mouth worked, but no words came out.

"I'll tell you what that is. You have to leave here and never come back. Don't ever show your face in this area again. If you do, they will hurt you, and I might not be around to protect you."

He stepped closer and ran his hand down the side of her face. She stood there, still in shock, afraid to move, breathing rapidly, her heart beating fiercely in her chest.

"You remember that little pre-nup you signed before we were married? You get nothing, you know. You came with nothing, and you will leave with nothing. I have decided you can keep the car. You need something to drive away from here in and never return. I want the credit cards back, though. You've survived with less, and I'm sure you will again."

Jim stood back, and Laura finally got the nerve to move toward the car. The pain in her ankle was excruciating, but she was aware of it only in a strange, detached sort of way. She fumbled in her backpack and pulled out her keys. Her hands trembled as Jim watched her open the door and retrieve her purse. She pulled out the wallet and handed him the cards.

"The checkbook too," he commanded.

She handed him the checkbook without the slightest hesitation. Then they stood and looked at each other. A moment passed; they both saw what they had, and both felt a twinge of the love they had once felt. But they also knew the impossibility of them ever being together again. Laura wanted desperately to tell Jim that she was sorry and that part of this had been her fault. On the other hand, if he hadn't been so ruthless, none of this would have ever happened. Years of keeping her emotions bottled up inside her would not permit her to speak her mind.

Laura broke into tears, a rush of emotions finally pouring forth in an unstoppable flow. She looked at Jim through her tears and tried to remember him as he had been, at least what her perception of him had been. She climbed into the car, thankful that at least he let her take it, and before she closed the door, she softly said, "I'm sorry, Jim—not for what I did, but for how things turned out." That was all she had to say.

"Good luck, Laura. Write to me when you get where you are going so I can send the divorce papers."

He turned without looking back. He seemed to have already put his past behind him as he headed back down the trail, looking only ahead.

# Chapter 14

ONCE LAURA HAD DRIVEN THE car back onto the dirt and found her way to the main road, she pulled the car to the curb and cried. Her body was in a complete state of shock. She couldn't decide which was worse, the pain in her chest or the pain in her ankle. She let herself cry in deep, soul-wrenching sobs. Her world was now turned upside down again—not an unfamiliar feeling in her life, just an extremely unpleasant one. She tried to be thankful for the year she had with Jim before she knew what he was really like, and she tried to be thankful that at least she could return to her aunt. She was almost thankful that she did not find Alex, although his presence would have been a comfort. She didn't feel like she could take care of anyone right now, including herself. At least the dog was learning to adapt and survive in his new environment. That was something she had learned to do, but she'd never wanted to have to do it again. She was going to have to start all over, and the prospect made her feel old and tired beyond her years.

She picked her head up and reached over to search her glove box for a tissue to wipe her eyes and blow her nose. As she did, an envelope fell out of the compartment. It had her name on it in Jim's handwriting. She opened it and found some money and a note.

Laura,

I felt guilty about leaving you with nothing, so here is some cash to get you through until you can get settled. Please don't try to contact me because we both know that our marriage is over. Here is the address of our lawyer. Send him your address as soon as you get one. Sorry things did not work out. You are beautiful, and I think we would have made a great team. Take care of yourself.

Jim


Laura wanted to throw the cash out the window, but she knew she would need it in order to survive this ordeal. Jim had obviously brought the spare key and while he was waiting for her placed the envelope where she was bound to find it. She wondered why he hadn't just taken his credit cards and the checkbook, but only briefly. It was his form of revenge to humiliate her by forcing her to physically hand everything over to him, and he'd also needed a forum to deliver his speech. She had to smile a little as she realized how humiliated he must have been when the boys came back and gave him the news that his estranged wife had tricked them into blowing the job. Feeling some of her anger return and push away some of the pain, Laura got her strength back to continue the drive. At least this time, she knew the way to her aunt's house.

Glancing at her gas gauge, she realized that she was on empty. Instead of turning back up the mountain, she felt she'd better head down and try one of the exits for a town on the way back to the city. The small stations up the mountain were unreliable and far and few between. And at least if she ran out of gas, there was traffic in this direction and a better chance of someone assisting her.

"Great, this is all I need. One more problem to deal with, one more slap in the face," she said to herself out loud. *Watch me run out of gas and have Jim and the goons drive by me while I am trapped like a sitting duck on the side of the road.*

She tried not to look at the gas gauge, but her eyes kept straying and noticing the white needle pinned to the edge of the red warning area, subtly sliding into the red zone. She tried to coast down as much of the mountain as possible, but eventually the road flattened out and she had to use her precious gas. Laura saw a sign appear in the distance, providing the distance to the next few exits. About that time, the engine sputtered, and with it the last of Laura's reserves.

"Damn, damn, damn it to hell!" Laura cried, pounding on the wheel of the car as it coasted to the shoulder.

*Okay*, she told herself unconvincingly, *everything happens for a reason. I just don't know what that reason is yet.*

She sat there, trying to decide what to do. Her ankle throbbed again, and she didn't feel up to getting out of the car to flag down help. She was quite sure her cell phone was dead after several days in her purse. She knew she had to do something; time was of the essence.

She hobbled out of the car and slammed the door. Her ankle screamed in pain at being jolted. *Well, at least this time I have some money.*

Traffic was sparse, and no one seemed to be in a hurry to stop and inquire if she needed help, even though her emergency flashers signaled a problem. Once again, she was filthy and her clothes were torn. She looked down at the stains on her jacket; the shoulder she had rolled on was covered with grass stains and dirt. Her jeans were ripped on one knee, and there was dirt ground into the fabric. She thought about trying to brush herself off, but that would be an exercise in futility. She briefly considered climbing into the backseat and changing her clothes so at least she wouldn't look so bedraggled, which might improve her chances of someone offering to help her. However, she didn't think she could manage changing her clothes in the confined area considering the bulkiness of her makeshift splint and her ankle being in so much pain.

She stood there, hoping someone would just stop and put her out of her misery. Then, in a déjà vu moment, she thought she saw a very familiar truck appear on the horizon. She blinked and looked down and then looked again to make sure she was seeing correctly. She didn't quite believe her eyes at first, but coming down the highway was a dark blue truck she recognized pulling a silver horse trailer. She hobbled toward the road, still not believing it was possible, and waved frantically. The truck slowed down and approached her car. To her astonishment, the rig pulled to the curb in front of her, the haunches of two horses resting against the tailgate as the trailer pulled to a gentle stop. Out of the truck, the man she had met on this same road only a week before stepped out. Nick was just as surprised, if not more so, to see her.

"Laura, is that you?"

"Nick, am I glad to see you!"

She suddenly felt her face flush with embarrassment over having him see her filthy and stranded on the side of the highway for a second time. She knew her eyes were still red from crying.

"Are you hurt?" he asked immediately, furrowing his brow and looking her over from head to toe.

All she could do was nod as he walked up to her and wrapped her in a bear hug. She flung her arms around the virtual stranger and swooned in pain and fatigue. He held her as she sobbed uncontrollably into his shoulder, her mental and physical pain released in choking breaths. Feeling her weakness, he carefully lifted her, his strong back and biceps easily carrying her weight to the truck. He lifted her to reach the handle on his pickup, and she swung the door open. Gently, he placed her on the roomy bench seat of the truck. She swung around and elevated her foot immediately to try to ease some of the pain screaming from her ankle.

Nick walked around to the other side of the truck and climbed in, shutting off the truck's engine.

"Do you make it a habit of stranding yourself along this highway on a weekly basis?" Nick asked in a mocking but serious manner.

Laura had to smile at the irony. Between sniffs of her running nose, she replied, "And do you make it a habit of rescuing stranded women along this highway on a weekly basis?"

"I guess I do now, although I have to admit you seem to be my most frequent customer. What happened this time?"

"I was out in the same woods looking for my dog, and I slipped on some rocks and hurt my ankle. Then I had the great fortune to run out of gas on my way home. Now is that so hard to believe?"

"No," Nick replied, "no harder to believe than me running into you twice on the same stretch of highway. I just happened to go back and get two more horses from the same farm I got the others from last week. Otherwise, I never drive down this road. But I can't help but admit that as I was driving down this road I was thinking about our first meeting. When I saw you by the side of the road, I couldn't believe it was really you. I thought it was a just some woman who looked a lot like you. Now let me take a look at your ankle. I am a healer, you know. It's just that I am used to working on patients who have a lot hairier legs than yours."

Laura laughed despite the pain. "I don't know about that. I haven't shaved for over a week," she admitted with some embarrassment.

Nick gently took her foot in his lap to examine her ankle, but Laura stopped him.

"Nick, I have to be honest about something. I could be putting you in danger. There are some people looking for me, and they want to hurt me. I don't want to get you involved in all of this."

"Let me guess. The lost puppy police have a warrant out for your arrest because you violated the leash law on your last camping trip? What could you possibly have done to get 'these people' so angry at you?" Nick probed.

"It is a long story, one I probably don't have the time to go into detail about. I want you to know that I didn't do anything illegal, but I broke up some big plans that involved a lot of money. Let's just say that they are not happy about it. Anyway, they will be headed down this same road fairly soon, I think. I need to get gas in my car and get out of here."

"You also need to get to an emergency room and have this ankle looked at," Nick added.

"*No!*" Laura exclaimed. "I can't go to the emergency room right now. My ankle will be fine. I just need to get out of here."

Nick took both of her hands in his and then paused as he noticed the wedding band and diamond ring. "Laura, I know this is none of my business, but where is your husband in all of this. Why isn't he protecting you?"

Laura pulled her hands away from Nick, uncomfortable about sharing that detail, but feeling she owed it to Nick to be honest with him. She crossed her arms and stared up in the air, taking a deep breath of frustration.

"He is one of the people involved in all of this, and one of the people who want to hurt me."

"Why don't you call the police?" Nick asked. His hands rose, emphasizing his concern.

"I don't have any evidence. They are part of a big corporation, and I am one individual."

"Fine, give me a minute, and we'll get you the heck out of here," Nick stated as he reached for his cell phone. Within a few minutes he had made some calls and arranged for a tow truck to come get Laura's car and take it to a station in a nearby town. He then reached into a medical kit in the backseat of the truck and pulled a large pill out of a bottle. Laura stared at it with large eyes and then felt better when he broke the pill in half and handed it to her.

"Don't worry. It is horse medicine but I take it all the time. It will reduce the swelling and help with the pain until I can get you into my office to get some X-rays."

"Your office?" Laura sounded surprised.

"What else am I going to do with you? You won't go to the emergency room, and you can't go home. I could get into a lot of trouble for practicing medicine on you, but I don't think you will rat me out."

"Wait," Laura blurted out. "There are some things I need from my car. Would you please get my backpack and my purse?" She remembered she had put the envelope with the money in her purse.

"Sure, no problem, as long as I am not at risk for a drive-by shooting on my way to your car," he chided, turning to grin at her.

Laura laughed again. She was amazed that this man could arrive like a knight in shining armor and rescue her and make her laugh. An hour ago, she thought she would never laugh again.

Nick returned with the items she had requested, started the truck, and pulled back onto the highway. The horses thumped a bit; they had relaxed during their wait and then had to rebalance as the truck pulled onto the highway. Nick pulled out the same red thermos she had seen on her first ride with him.

"You need something to drink to take that pill."

She hadn't even realized she was still gripping the pill in her hand. She poured some coffee into the red lid and swallowed the bitter-tasting medicine. The pill, even cut in half, was huge, and it felt as if it were lodged in her throat. She took another big swallow of the warm liquid and forced the pill down her esophagus and into her stomach. She hoped she would feel its effects soon.

"Well," Nick remarked, "we have a long drive before we reach my clinic. Why don't you start at the beginning? "

Laura was feeling the effects of the medication when they arrived at the town Nick called home. They drove through the small but quaint little town and then into the countryside a few miles. Nick's office was a picturesque building with a few acres on each side fenced into small paddocks. Each paddock had a lean-to; some were occupied by lonely-looking horses, others empty, waiting for the next patient. Nick pulled the trailer into the circular stone driveway and immediately jumped out to assist Laura. The medication had eased her pain tremendously; Laura had even considered getting out and walking into the office.

"Don't you even think about it," Nick warned as he stopped her from getting out of the truck. He came around to the door she had already opened and lifted her once again into his arms. He carried her to the front door. As she reached for the handle, a woman in her early twenties wearing a white lab coat opened the door. She looked shocked as Nick carried Laura past her.

"Do me a favor, Ester. Unload the two horses and put them in an empty paddock. They shouldn't give you any trouble."

Nick carried Laura into a back room and placed her on a hard, flat table. She giggled, a bit tipsy from the meds.

"I don't think your associate quite knew what to make of the situation," Laura observed. "I'll bet it is not every day that you carry in patients of the two-legged variety."

"I'll explain the situation later, or at least give her a reasonable explanation that will satisfy her curiosity."

Removing her makeshift splint carefully, Nick examined and prodded Laura's ankle. He remained professional as he asked, "Does this hurt?" several different times. Laura felt confident that he had a good knowledge of human anatomy and would diagnose her properly.

"You should have been a doctor," she observed.

"Definitely not. People complain too much."

"I haven't complained, have I?" she asked, suddenly feeling very sleepy on the hard white table.

"No, you are a good patient. And you were right about your legs being hairy. Just saying. You have hairier legs than a goat I treated this week."

Laura giggled hysterically, slightly embarrassed. She closed her eyes sleepily.

"I'm just kidding about the hairy leg thing," Nick confessed. "You go ahead and close your eyes. I can take the X-rays with my portable machine. You won't feel a thing."

Laura closed her eyes and heard Nick walk out of the room. He returned, and she felt a heated blanket being draped over her and another placed under her head, like a pillow. She knew the exhaustion and the medication had finally overcome her. She wanted to drift off on those fluffy clouds and sleep.

As she drifted off, she heard a woman's voice call to Nick. She entered the room. Two sets of footsteps walked back out into the hallway, and she heard quiet arguing in the doorway. It was the familiar kind of quarreling between two people who knew each other well; the raised whispers of equals, not of a boss explaining a situation to an employee. There was judgment in the woman's voice and defense in his. The last thought Laura had as she drifted off was that she hoped she had not caused any trouble for Nick.

When she awoke, Laura was stiff from lying on her back on the hard table. She sat up and wondered what time it was. She looked down at her foot and saw a plaster cast encasing her leg. Her guess was that she had broken it. Apparently, Nick had been so gentle that he had managed to put the cast on while she was asleep. She listened carefully but didn't hear any voices coming from anywhere in the building.

"Nick," she called out uncertainly.

"I'm coming," his voice returned.

She was glad to know she hadn't been abandoned in the office by herself.

Nick appeared in the room, now in a white lab coat. "And how is my number-one patient doing this evening?"

"This evening?" Laura responded, somewhat surprised. It had been early afternoon when they arrived at the clinic.

"Yes, evening. It is 8:30 p.m. as we speak. You should be well rested after your little nap. I guess those meds really knocked you out. Sorry about that. It doesn't affect me that way."

"That's okay. I probably needed the sleep. I didn't feel a thing after you wrapped me up in those warm blankets."

"Aren't they nice? We keep blankets in a warmer for the animals after they have had surgery or if they come in traumatized and in shock."

"Speaking of shock," Laura interrupted. "What is the news on the ankle, doc?"

"You have a clean hairline fracture, which means a cast and a few weeks off the leg, and then you should be good as new. You are lucky you didn't displace the fractured bone, hiking through the woods on it. You must have done a good job with that splint."

"I guess you wouldn't happen to have any crutches available. Most of your patients don't require crutches, do they?"

"No, I don't have any here, but Ester said she had a pair from an injury from playing basketball in high school. She volunteered to go home and see if she could find them."

"That's really nice of her. How is she taking the news that you treated me for a broken ankle?"

"I told you I would handle the situation, and I did. She is fine with this, really. Don't worry about it."

Laura could detect something in the tone of his voice that sounded less than convincing.

"Are you hungry?" he asked her. "I ordered some pizza while you were out—I mean asleep. I meant to say, out like a light."

Laura smiled at his awkwardness. He had seemed so self-assured and confident during the time they had been together. All of a sudden, now he seemed vulnerable. It was as if he thrived on crisis situations, but when it came to one-on-one, being comfortable around the opposite sex was not his forte.

"That depends," Laura answered. "Do I have to spend another minute on this rock-hard table, or am I allowed to move and eat the pizza somewhere more comfortable?"

"Oh my God, I am so sorry. I told you, this is why I like my animal patients. They never complain that my table is too hard."

Nick moved to Laura's side and eased her off the table. "I don't want you walking on this cast, so you are going to have to lean on me and use me as a crutch until we get to my office. It is a lot more comfortable in there."

Nick gripped Laura around the waist. Laura wrapped her arms around his broad shoulders. He was warm and solid.

Nick was careful not to look directly at her as they shuffled down the hallway toward his office. "I spend a lot of time here, sometimes overnight, so I have made my office fairly livable."

The office was not large but held a couch, a few chairs, a desk, and a small fridge in the corner. The walls were decorated with a few framed pictures of hunting dogs, and his framed veterinary certificates hung above his desk. Nick helped Laura to the couch and helped her elevate the ankle. He retrieved a pillow and a blanket from the closet and placed the pillow under her leg and draped the blanket over her lap. He then went to the fridge and got a bottle of water and some ibuprofen from a bottle in his desk and brought those back to her as well.

"How is the pain? You should take these," he said, handing her the pills.

"The pain is much better, down to a dull roar. Such service at this fine healing clinic," Laura said, grateful for the kindness Nick was showing her. "I just hope I can afford your services. I don't have any insurance, you know. I'm sure my husband has already taken me off the policy."

Nick dragged a chair and folding table over to the couch and then placed a box of delicious-smelling pizza on the table in front of her. "I'm sure we can work something out. I'll have you clean stalls to pay off your bill, as soon as you can walk without crutches."

Laura took a slice of the warm pizza, dripping with various toppings and extra cheese. She was hungrier than she realized and savored each mouthful, trying not to make a pig out of herself in front of Nick.

"Where are my manners?" Nick exclaimed suddenly. He stood and walked to his fridge. "Let's see what I have to drink. I have iced tea. I make it at home in these saline bottles. I know it looks like urine samples, but actually, my tea is pretty darned good. I also have a couple of beers. They are for after hours, of course."

Laura laughed, finding Nick's attempts to make her comfortable endearing. "You just got me a drink, but I think I would like some tea." Nick did not know about her past and her revulsion to the smell of beer.

Just then, the door to the building opened, and Ester breezed in like a draft of cold air. Her blonde hair was pulled into a tight ponytail. The tails of her white lab coat fluttered excitedly behind her. She halted abruptly and set down the pair of crutches she had been carrying. She stood there, looking at Laura, waiting unpretentiously for an introduction.

"Ester, meet Laura. Laura, this is Ester," Nick said in an almost mocking tone.

It was clear to Laura that there was some tension, and she wondered what the relationship was between them. She hadn't felt it was appropriate to ask Nick that question.

"I'd get up and shake your hand, but ..." Laura started.

"Nice to meet you, Laura," Ester interrupted in a sweet, melodic accent.

Laura could tell that beneath the lab coat was a very attractive woman whose physical appearance matched the beauty of her voice.

"Would you like to sit down and have some pizza with us?" Nick offered.

"No, thank you. I have some work to do at home. I'll see you later," she stated rather pointedly. She turned and left the room as abruptly as she had entered.

"Thank you for the crutches," Laura yelled after her. "Is that your wife?" Laura finally asked. She didn't know why, but she was very relieved when he answered no.

"We have been together so long we don't know what we are anymore. All I know is that she is afraid of letting me go. She knows that our arrangement was never meant to be permanent, but our lives are so intertwined that separating us would be like trying to separate a tree from its roots."

"You don't have to share this with me if you don't want to," Laura offered.

"I'm kind of enjoying it. After all, you've shared your life with me today. Shouldn't I reciprocate? I feel after everything we have been through together, I hope that we are friends."

"I'm sorry, please continue," Laura said apologetically.

"Anyway, she is much too young for me, and she latched on even though I told her not to because I would end up hurting her. She is kind of like a pit bull. Now that she feels she has me in her jaws, she doesn't want to let me go. And to be truthful, I haven't given her a reason," Nick confessed. Then he looked over at Laura and smiled and said, "Until now."

Laura blushed and smiled but could not lift her gaze to meet Nick's. Butterflies danced in her stomach. Laura took another slice of pizza, and then asked, "What do you mean, till now?"

Nick and Laura talked until midnight. They talked about the things they liked about people and the things they disliked about people. They delved into one another's thoughts, probing each other's minds and sending feelers out to test the sensitivity of each other's feelings. They liked what they saw in one another and felt a commonality in their emotional needs and desires. But there were still barriers between them that separated them from getting too close. For Nick, it was an unfinished relationship with someone he did not love but he cared very deeply about. For Laura, it was the pain that she recently endured, the losses she had suffered, and the uncertainty that she now faced. They were two ships that passed in the night, and both knew that the timing was wrong for developing their relationship. They both had business to attend to, although Laura's task seemed the greater of the two.

It was sometime after midnight, the remaining pizza long since cold and hardened in the box, when Nick confessed that he'd better return home or there might be hell to pay in the morning.

"Are you sure you will be all right here alone?" Nick asked Laura.

"Just leave the ibuprofen where I can reach it and I will be fine. Leave the bathroom light on so if I have to use it in the middle of the night I won't break my other ankle."

"The clinic opens at nine. I will be back here by eight thirty to open up. I have a few rounds to make tomorrow morning, but after I finish I can take you back to your car."

"I don't want you driving all that way back to my car," Laura told him with genuine concern. "You've done more for me than I can ever repay. I'll take a bus or some type of public transportation and not put you out any more than I already have."

Nick sat down next to her on the couch and tucked the blanket around her. He brushed the hair off her face and kissed her tenderly on the forehead.

"Please let me drive you?" he asked softly. "I would really like a couple of more hours of your company before you walk out of my life."

Laura was touched by his feelings for her, and although her own feelings were still numb from the breakup with Jim, she could sense that if things had been different …

"Sure, I would love your company for a few more hours," she returned sleepily.

Nick sat next to her for a little while, watching her sleep. He stared at her as if he were trying to memorize every line of her face, the gentle curves of her mouth, and each detail of her delicate features. Then he rose, turned out the lights, and went home to Ester.

# Chapter 15

Laura woke up long before anyone came into the office the following morning. She was ahead on her quota for sleep because of the long nap she had taken the day before. Her internal alarm clock woke her up around six. She sat up, feeling the need to use the bathroom. The crutches had been placed beside the couch, ready for her to use should she need them. Laura suspected that they were adjusted incorrectly for her height; she didn't think Ester was as tall as she, and Ester had probably been much shorter in high school than she was now. When Laura lowered her leg to the floor, the dull throb turned up several notches, and she realized she needed to take more ibuprofen as well as use the bathroom. She pulled herself up to a standing position on her good foot and positioned the crutches under her armpits. As she expected, they were too short, but she decided they would have to do until she took care of the necessities.

Taking a few unsure steps, Laura tested out the technique of walking with crutches; she had never used them before. She got the hang of it within a few steps and confidently moved forward, even though she was hunched over because they were too low. Her backpack was lying on the floor near the end of the couch, and Laura decided to tote it with her to the bathroom and attempt a much-needed clothes change while she was there. She balanced herself, both crutches in one hand, and picked up the backpack. Transferring the backpack to her shoulder and a crutch to the other hand, she started for the bathroom. As she tried to squeeze between the couch and the card table, the trailing edge of the backpack caught the corner of the card table. The table fell, and Laura watched helplessly as the box containing the remains of the pizza, the beer bottles, and tea glass from the previous evening tumbled to the floor. Each bottle rolled in a different direction and of course the pizza spilled out of the box and ended up facedown on the floor.

"Oh, great!" Laura exclaimed out loud. "Now I've gone and wrecked the place."

She decided to concentrate on one task at a time, so she headed for the bathroom to heed the call of nature, wash, and change her clothes. She'd come back and clean up the mess. She didn't feel rushed because it was only six in the morning and Nick would not be there for another two hours.

Laura made it successfully to the bathroom. She brushed her teeth and used a washcloth and hand towel to give herself a sponge bath. She did her best to wash her hair in the large sink and used some of her camping soap to make herself feel human again. Then she looked down at her pants. They were dirty and ripped, and Nick had been forced to make a cut along the leg to put on the cast. She contemplated how she was going to get the old jeans off and her clean pair on. Sitting on the edge of the toilet, she pulled the pants down past her waist and easily pulled the good leg out. Getting the other leg out was going to be more difficult because she needed someone to pull the cut end gently over her cast. Laura was not happy with the idea of cutting one of her last remaining pairs of jeans, but it looked as if she didn't have any other choice. What she really needed at the moment was a pair of scissors. She was afraid to use her camping knife to cut so closely to her skin.

Trying to think of a solution to her dilemma, she figured that Nick would have a pair of scissors somewhere back in the room where he put on her cast. She could cut the pants she was wearing all the way off, which would make them easy to remove, and then work on slitting her other jeans enough to get them on over the cast.

Instead of using the crutches, Laura decided to travel back through the office to the operating room on her hands and knees. Her pants were half-on and half-off, and she needed to carry the other pair with her. She was afraid that the dragging pair of pants would get caught up in the crutches and trip her. Throwing the clean pair of pants over her shoulder, Laura gingerly got down on her hands and knees and crawled out of the bathroom, making sure her cast did not bang against the floor. She found herself to be quite adept at moving around, but she was glad that no one was around to see her in this position. The throb in her ankle reminded her that she needed to take the ibuprofen, so she decided to detour to the office and take the medicine before she worked on cutting off her pants. She remembered the iced tea in the fridge and thought she would use it to swallow the pills. Crawling to the fridge, she reached to get the clear plastic saline bottle Nick used to make and store his own brand of iced tea. Resting on her knees, she reached into the fridge to grab the bottle. Unfortunately, she didn't count on the shooting pain radiating from her ankle when she put her full weight on her knee and foot. Doubling over from the pain, Laura involuntarily grabbed the rack of the fridge to take the weight off her knee. The rack, however, was not secured in the back, and it tipped forward, immediately emptying the rack holding several containers of tea, the few beers that were left, and an open container of half-and-half onto the floor.

Laura cringed, not only from the pain but the accumulation of debris that now joined the pizza and beer from her first disaster. She had single-handedly trashed Nick's office. Convinced the situation was not beyond salvaging, she untangled herself from the dragging jeans and turned around on her hands and knees to retrieve the refrigerator items, and then take her ibuprofen. She planned to continue to the operating room and get the scissors and remove her pants. She felt as if things were not that bad, still under control, until she heard the door to the clinic open and someone walk into the building.

"Oh my God!" Laura exclaimed in horror. Before she could move, Nick and Ester walked into the office.

They both came to an abrupt stop at the doorway and took in the scene before them. Laura was posed on her hands and knees in a T-shirt and underwear, jeans hanging from one leg. The door to the fridge was wide open, all the contents spilled on the floor, including the half-and-half, which lay on its side, slowly leaking its thick white liquid onto the floor. The card table was overturned, beer bottles strewn into various corners of the office, and half a pizza lay facedown on the floor, half covered by the empty box.

Laura was speechless.

"And I thought you'd still be asleep," Nick remarked to Laura's horrified expression. "Who could have guessed you'd already be up and wrecking the place?"

Laura did not know what to say. She had never been so embarrassed in her entire life.

"I can explain!"

"I'm sure I am going to love this story, but a patient is on the way in, needing my immediate attention. Why don't I close the door and let you go back to destroying the place? When I am done with the emergency, I will be back for a chat."

Nick couldn't help but smile as he closed the door, knowing full well that he was adding more discomfort to an obviously embarrassing situation. He was sure she had been through a series of unpreventable accidents, but he honestly didn't have the time to stick around and help. The moment the horse arrived, he and Ester would be busy stitching it up, and they needed to prepare immediately.

Ester glared at Nick with an "I told you this woman was trouble" look, but Nick cut her off before she had a chance to speak.

"Ester, get the sutures and tranquilizers ready and meet me in the back room."

The room in the back was a converted garage that could accommodate working on horses indoors without actually having to bring them into the clinic.

"I'll prepare a warm bucket of water and Betadine and grab the wraps and bandages." Ester couldn't help walking away with the comment, "That woman is an accident waiting to happen, Nick, and I can't believe you brought her here."

Nick didn't answer her but turned and went to get his supplies.

Back in the office, Laura was desperately trying to rectify her horrifying situation. First, she crawled back to the bathroom to her backpack. She grabbed her hunting knife and, without any regard for her safety, cut the jeans off her leg. Next, she took her other jeans and ripped down the inside seam from the knee down. The cut was jagged, but she didn't care at that point. She jammed her aching casted foot through the pant leg. She pulled the pants up and zipped and buttoned them; then she retrieved her crutches and went back to the disaster area with some paper towels. She straightened out the refrigerator shelf and replaced the fallen items. Next, she mopped up the spilled half-and-half and then proceeded to clean up each item. She shoveled the overturned pizza back into the box and wiped up the floor. She found a trash can in which to deposit the box, but the box was too large for the opening. She bent the box in half, with the pizza still in it, and forced it into the opening with a vengeance. The remaining beer bottles were easy to collect and put in a recyclable container. She glanced around for any remaining spills or messes that needed to be cleaned up and, finally satisfied, dragged herself back to the couch for a rest. She grabbed the ibuprofen and swallowed three pills without any liquid. They felt like rocks going down her throat. She wondered how a day could become such a disaster by seven in the morning. By the time Nick and Ester returned, at least she would have all her clothes on and the mess would be cleaned up. There was no telling when they were going to return.

Back in the garage, Nick finished the last suture on the horse's fragile legs. The damage had been repaired to the best of his ability; now it was up the horse's body to heal the wounds. He'd covered the stitches with a soft gauze bandage, followed by a layer of supportive wraps. A temporary standing stall was already prepared in the corner of the garage, kept in readiness for horses that needed to remain immobile after surgery. When the horse was ready to take a few steps, still groggy from the tranquilizer, Nick carefully guided it into the stall. Fresh sections of hay waited in the hay rack, and a bucket of clean water was in easy reach of the horse. Nick asked Ester to stay with the horse for a few minutes while he came out from under the effects of the tranquilizer. He handed her a syringe and instructed her to administer it if the horse became agitated. It was important that the horse remain as immobile as possible for the next few days to ensure proper healing.

Nick walked out into the growing morning light to discuss his prognosis for the horse's recovery with the owners. While he could not guarantee the horse would recover completely, the odds were in his favor. The owners smiled at Nick and thanked him for his outstanding efforts and for his emergency services, but as usual Nick sent them on their way, telling them to go home and get some rest after their trying experience. They could discuss the bill later.

Laura was bent over her crutches, trying to change the adjustments on them, when Nick knocked softly on the door and entered the office. Laura had been rehearsing what she was going to say to Nick when he entered the room. She was immediately relieved to see that Ester was not with him, because having her around made the situation even more tense than it already was.

"I hope you'll give me a chance to explain what you saw this morning," she burst out before Nick had a chance to speak. "I woke up early and knocked into the table with the crutches. I was going to clean it up, but I had to use the bathroom, and then I got my pants stuck over the cast so I crawled out to look for scissors," she continued, pausing for a breath. "Then I went to the fridge to get something to take the ibuprofen with, and I accidentally knocked over the shelf. That was when you walked in and saw me with my pants down," she concluded in the tone of an admonished child getting caught with her hand in the cookie jar.

Nick walked over and sat down on the couch next to her. "I'm sorry I had to walk out on you so quickly this morning, but I had an emergency that I had to tend to immediately. I realize it must have been difficult for you not being able to explain yourself when I left," he said, compassion in his voice.

"I guess you could say that," she replied, suddenly realizing that she had a reason to feel agitated as well as embarrassed. She had not even considered that Nick's actions might have been at fault, only hers. He was apologizing, so she decided to play along. After all, it was better to be on the offensive than it was to be on the defensive.

"I had to sit here for over an hour and stew about the two of you walking into the office two hours before you said you would be here. If you had come in at eight thirty like you said, I wouldn't have been caught in that embarrassing situation. Now your girlfriend thinks I'm nuts!"

"All I can say in my defense is that emergencies happen. I didn't plan to be up at six this morning. I would have loved to have slept in another two hours."

Laura felt bad about her verbal attack on Nick and watched as he strode over to his desk and shuffled meaninglessly through papers. He looked like a little boy pouting.

"Well then, if you are willing to forget that this ever happened and that you ever saw me on all fours with my pants down, then I'll forgive your early intrusion."

Smiling, Nick replied, "You've got a deal, lady. I'm just sorry all those things had to happen to you this early in the morning. I wish I could have been around to help you so that none of it happened."

"You've done enough for me, Dr. Jackson. You probably can't wait to get me out of your hair. Speaking of which, I still want you to consider my offer to take public transportation back to my car. I really hate to bother you again."

"Don't be ridiculous. You are like a bright ray of sunshine in my life," he said with honesty that Laura could see in his eyes. "I am going to go and complete my morning appointments, and then I am going to take you out to breakfast and back to your car—that is, only if I can't talk you into staying a couple of more days."

"I can't, Nick," Laura said, looking away from the lure of his intense gaze. "My aunt doesn't have a phone, and it isn't fair to worry her. She is expecting me back today. Besides that, I have some serious work to do to figure out what direction my life is headed from here."

"I understand," Nick said with resolution. "I know it is boring in here, but I will be back in an hour if you think you can wait that long."

"I'll be just fine. Maybe I'll lie back down and shut my eyes for a few minutes. All the frantic cleaning up I had to do this morning has tired me out already."

Nick laughed.

"All right then, you lie back down," Nick said as he helped her back on the couch and covered her with a blanket. "I'll be back before you know it."


Nick left the office and Laura allowed herself to relax into that place between awareness and sleep. Her mind drifted to past events. She thought about Jim and what he might be doing at that moment. She thought about her heartache from the tragic events that took place in the last week and the breath of fresh air Nick had been. She thought about her Aunt Gracie and how wonderful it was to have her back in her life. Then, just as she was about to cross over the conscious plane into the unconscious state of sleep, the door to the office opened. Laura sat up in surprise that Nick had returned so soon.

"I hope I didn't wake you," Ester said as she walked into the room. "I just thought I would come in and see if you needed any help. You looked like you might need some the last time I saw you," she said in her soft southern lilt.

Laura understood the real reason Ester had taken this opportunity to visit her when Nick was not there. She wanted to feel her out and find out if Laura had a hidden agenda that included stealing her man.

"I think I have everything under control, thank you. I managed to get things cleaned up on my own. Now I am just waiting for Nick to return so he can take me back to my car. You two have been so kind to let me stay here and help me with my injury."

She was careful to add the "you two" so Ester would feel that Laura considered them a couple.

"Well, since Nick is so busy this morning, why don't you let me run you back to your car so we don't have to bother him? His time is much too valuable to be running a shuttle service."

Laura started to respond and then realized she didn't know what to say. If she presented an argument over letting Ester drive her, she'd fuel her suspicions that Nick and she had feelings for one another. On the other hand, if she let Ester drive her, she might hurt Nick's feelings, plus she wouldn't be able to say good-bye to him. She decided to try another approach.

"I really don't think it is fair that you have to drive me. Besides, if you take me, I won't be able to thank Nick in person for all he has done for me this past week. After all, he took a risk treating me. The least I can do is thank him in person before I go. Also, Nick has agreed to let me take him out to breakfast when he returns, to thank him for his kindness. Maybe you would like to join us?"

Laura lied about Nick letting her take him out to breakfast, but in truth, she was going to insist on paying. She knew he would decline because he was a gentleman, but she felt it was less of lie because of her intentions.

The two women were locked in a battle, much like a chess game, each one carefully weighing the next move. They were each trying to think one move ahead of the other in order to achieve the upper hand. It was now Ester's turn in the intellectual battle.

"I really couldn't join you. One of us needs to be here around the clock to check on the horse Nick worked on this morning and in case of any other emergencies. We have a business to run that depends on our being here."

Laura could almost see the hairs on the back of Ester's neck rising. Her posture became tense, and Laura noticed her hands unconsciously curling into clenched fists.

"I don't think you realize how much of a burden you are placing on Nick right now. He is trying to run a practice, and you have him driving all over the country to suit your needs. What happens if there is an emergency while Nick is out chauffeuring you around? Not only does he have a patient right here that needs him, but if there are additional emergencies, you could be costing the life of an animal," Ester spat, her eyes narrowing, glaring at Laura.

Laura could tell that Ester's new tactic was to use anger and try to scare Laura into leaving Nick alone. Unfortunately for Ester, Laura trusted Nick too much to listen to her argument. Nick would have never offered to drive her if he thought he was placing anyone in jeopardy.

"I can understand why you are upset, Ester," Laura said, trying to sound as pleasant as possible, "but I think Nick is capable of making his own decisions. So why don't we just wait until he comes back? We can all talk about this together."

Laura remembered from a previous conversation with Nick that he had a back-up friend who went on call when Nick went out of the area. She knew Ester's ploy was to get her out of here before Nick returned or her plans would be ruined.

"Look, Laura," Ester replied. Using a last-ditch effort to try to persuade Laura to see her point, she said, "There is a bus station ten minutes down the road. I could have you down there in ten minutes and be back before anyone missed me. *And out of my hair for good*, she thought. "That would solve all of our problems. Then you wouldn't be responsible for Nick missing any emergencies."

Laura thought for a moment about how she could argue her way out of this proposal. If she truly had Nick's best interest in mind, then there wasn't a plausible reason for her not to take Ester up on her offer. She hated the thought of not being able to say good-bye to Nick and thank him again for all he had done for her. She sat still, several thoughts coursing through her mind at once.

"Well?"

Ester's voice startled her out of her trance.

"We can leave right now, and I'll be back in time to check on the horse. You can even write Nick a thank-you note in the car on the way to the bus station."

"Do you mind if I borrow your crutches?" Laura asked, stalling. "I can return them in a couple of weeks, I'm sure."

"You can keep them, honey. I doubt I will be needing them ever again," Ester responded quickly, emphasizing the "keep them."

"I'll need to use the bathroom one more time before I get on the bus, and I have to make sure I didn't leave anything behind," Laura said, hoping that Nick would return if she stalled long enough.

Ester leaned forward, inches from Laura, and raised her eyebrows as she said, "There's a restroom at the bus station. I'll check the bathroom for you." She rushed to the bathroom and gave a quick glance around, returning before Laura had her pack on. Ester seemed cheery with her victory and smiled as she informed Laura, "Nothing left behind. Let's be on our way so I can hurry back."

Laura slowly made her way to Ester's waiting car, which was parked in front of the clinic. She knew it was killing Ester to walk so slowly and suspected that Ester knew she was capable of moving more quickly but couldn't bring herself to rush an invalid. When they reached the car, Laura put the crutches in the backseat and sat up front with Ester. She kept glancing toward the road, hoping she would see Nick's truck pulling into the driveway. Even as they drove out of the clinic, Laura still hoped that Nick would prevent her from departing with Ester. Ester drove quickly, the wheels of the car emitting a faint squeal from the speedy turn onto the pavement. The two women drove in silence to the bus station. Laura knew Ester had won the victory, but she wondered what the consequences of this victory would have on her relationship with Nick. She knew that Nick would see this as interference in his life, unless Ester convinced him that Laura had voluntarily agreed to take the bus, which would only work if Laura and Nick did not communicate again. Laura could tell Ester was deep in thought; she stared at the road in front of her and drummed her fingers on the steering wheel.

As Ester had promised, it was a quick ride to the station. She unceremoniously deposited Laura, her backpack, and the crutches at the door to the small building where Laura would purchase her ticket and catch her bus, and Laura didn't know whether to thank her or yell at her for bringing her to the bus, so she said politely, "Good luck with everything."

Of course, Laura meant, *Good luck when Nick finds out what you've done to me, because you're going to need it.* The statement could have been construed to mean, "Good luck with the injured horse and your life with Nick." In any case, it was open-ended enough to depend on how Ester perceived the statement, and that was good enough for Laura. Ester didn't even have the courtesy to reply and drove off without a word, giving Laura a dismissive wave of her hand and a grin that Laura took to mean, "Checkmate."

Laura purchased a ticket to the town where Nick had instructed the tow truck to deposit her car. She was worried about paying the towing bill, which would eat into her shrinking supply of cash. She was jobless, almost moneyless, and the prospect of facing the uncertainties in her life suddenly seemed overwhelming. She sat on the hard bench outside the building to wait for her bus. Laura now wished she had summoned the strength to fight against Ester's wishes to remove her from Nick's life before they had a chance to strengthen the bond they had recently developed. But what right did she have to intrude into Ester's territory?

Laura had a difficult decision to make. She could ride out of this town and never contact Nick again. He didn't have an address for her, and he had absolutely no way of contacting her. Or she could return to the clinic and cause chaos in Nick and Ester's lives. Her third option was to get on the bus and, sometime in the future, after she had established herself, write to him and let him know where she was. If he was interested in pursuing their friendship, he would write back and let her know. Laura decided that the third option was the best. It wasn't fair to Nick to put him in a situation where he had to decide between her and Ester. He might not realize it now, but in time he would see the wisdom of her decision to leave as Ester had asked. She hoped.

Feeling better after thinking through the ramifications of her decision, Laura waited a few more minutes before the bus arrived. A nice young man heading back to college assisted her with boarding the bus and carried her backpack while she mounted the steep stairs, crutches in hand. The young man was eager to chat with her, but she politely withdrew to a seat away from him so she could spend the next couple of hours mindlessly melting into oblivion. She refused to think about anything distressing or painful or to make any plans for her future. She would have plenty of time to do that later. Her ankle still ached, and each time the bus hit a bump, she cringed in pain. She hated going back to face her aunt feeling like a failure, and on crutches to boot. But if there was anyone in the world who would understand how she felt right now, it would be her aunt. Laura was eagerly anticipating going to the only place she could call home and being smothered in her aunt's motherly love.

# *Chapter 16*

LAURA PULLED INTO HER AUNT'S driveway at dinnertime, three days after she had left. Her aunt immediately came flying out the door to greet her. As the car door opened and Laura's casted foot made its appearance, Gracie's expression of joy turned to horror.

"My child, what on earth did you do to yourself?" Gracie exclaimed.

"It's a long story, Aunt Gracie. Why don't we go inside and get something to eat, and I will tell you the whole story. I am starving. I haven't eaten since dinner last night."

In a rather subdued manner, Gracie noted, "I see you aren't returning with your little friend."

Laura hopped over to her aunt on one foot and threw her arms around her neck. "I was close this time. I found someone who thought he had seen Alex, but I wasn't able to go look for him," she whispered in her aunt's ear as she hugged her. She was once again very close to tears.

Gracie assisted Laura into the house, where Laura immediately smelled the aromas of good things to eat drifting from the kitchen. Gracie helped Laura onto the couch and rested her foot on a pillow. She disappeared and then returned with a TV tray to set beside Laura.

"Consider me your maid for the next week or so. I am going to wait on you hand and foot until I spoil you rotten. It was my idea for you to go into those woods alone, and now look what I've gone and made you do."

"Don't be ridiculous," Laura replied. "This accident had nothing to do with me looking for the dog. Some bad people were after me, and they are responsible for me hurting myself."

"Some people hurt you?" Gracie asked with surprise.

121

"They didn't hurt me directly," Laura explained. "I will fill you in on the details after we eat dinner."

"I'm so sorry, child. What am I thinkin'? Here you are, starving, and I am botherin' you with a hundred questions. Eat your dinner, and then we'll have a nice hot cup of tea. I baked some cookies for you, of course. Then you can catch me up on everythin' that happened."

Gracie had fixed Laura a delicious dinner of sweet potatoes and mashed potatoes, baked chicken, greens, and homemade biscuits. Laura closed her eyes when she was eating. She could almost pretend she was ten years old again, sitting down with her family to Sunday dinner at Aunt Gracie's house. Those were the only pleasant memories she had of her childhood, and even before the drive home, things would start to deteriorate. So she was content to be here now, at her present age, with the present company, and enjoy the wonderful food and her comfortable surroundings. Aunt Gracie was too anxious to wait till Laura finished her meal to hear about her adventures, so during the course of the meal, Laura recounted the trip from the time she left until the bus ride home.

Each time Laura came to a poignant moment, Gracie would interject a "Lordy" or an "Oh my," but for the most part she was content to sit and listen to the story unfold. When Gracie knew the story was completed, she asked a few questions.

"Do you think you would like to see this man Nick again someday?"

Laura didn't even have to think about the answer. "Of course I would, Aunt Gracie. He is everything I've always wanted in a man. He is kind, intelligent, down-to-earth, and considerate. But like I told you, he is in a relationship with someone right now, and my breakup is still too new to consider getting involved again so soon. I don't think I'll be able to trust my heart to anyone for a very long time."

"I know how you feel, darlin'," Gracie revealed. "I was married once a very long time ago, before you was even born."

Laura remembered her mother mentioning that she had an uncle, but the memory hadn't surfaced until just now, when Gracie brought up the subject.

"What was he like, and what happened to him?" Laura wanted to know, all at once.

"He was a very kind man. He was strong and handsome and he worked hard to make a livin'. Unfortunately, he worked in the mines, and the coal dust gave him cancer and he died. He had been workin' in those mines since he was fifteen years old. He never finished high school, so he always thought of himself as stupid. But I saw brilliance in him that no one else ever saw."

Laura listened with fascination. She was learning about a part of her family for the first time—and by the sound of it, a part of her family she could finally be proud of. She listened without interruption and let her aunt unfold the details of her story.

"He built this house for me, you know, all by himself. He chopped down every tree and built each rafter and joined each log of this cabin. This home was a labor of love. Each day he would come home from work and he would build a little more, even after puttin' in a twelve-hour day at the mine. He would manage to come home and work on somethin'. We had a little trailer that we lived in while he was buildin' this place. And while he was buildin', I would dream of what the house would look like when it was all finished. And all the while he was workin' so hard, that awful disease was eating away at his lungs. He never complained, even though he had to stop workin' because his coughin' got to be so bad. I knew he was ill, but he refused to go to a doctor. He had his pride, and he also knew there wasn't a thing they could do for him. We only lived in the house together for a year before he died. Once he went down, the rest came quickly, thank God. He wasn't a man to lie around in bed. To him, that was the worst part about dyin', the layin' around and waitin'."

They both sat in silence for a moment.

"I'm so sorry, Aunt Gracie," Laura finally managed to say. "I think my mother told me about him, but I didn't remember you even had a husband until now."

"Don't be sorry, child. I feel fortunate for the wonderful years we did have together. He gave me this home, and the insurance from all his years of hard work has allowed me to live comfortably. In a way, he is still takin' care of me. But the point I wanted to make is that I know how long it takes to heal a broken heart. The right man never came along again for me after your uncle, although several tried to fill his shoes. But somehow, I don't think that your heart will be broken forever. Jim was not the true love of your life, not with the way your marriage ended. When you do find the right person, there is somethin' so permanent about your love that this short lifetime here on earth isn't long enough to even begin to wear it down. My love for your uncle is still as strong as the last day we were together, and I know in my heart we will be together again someday."

Laura listened to her aunt's words of wisdom. "I guess you are probably right. I think I am feeling more numb than anything else. My life seemed to be so on track—everything seemed to be just perfect for once in my miserable life."

"Did it really," her aunt interrupted, "or were you just foolin' yourself into thinkin' so?"

"I don't think I can answer that right now. Maybe in time I will know the answer. All I know now is that my life has been turned upside down, and I don't know what to do. At least before I met Jim I had a job and a place to live. Now I don't even have that."

"You do have a place to live," her aunt pointed out. "You are more than welcome to stay here with me," she offered kindly.

"Thank you, Aunt Gracie. You are so kind and generous. But this is only temporary. I could never live in this town again. There are too many bad memories. I can stay here until I recover and can find a job and get on my feet at least. Just knowing that is a tremendous help in all of this uncertainty I have to face."

Gracie rose from the couch and smiled knowingly at Laura. She patted her knee and then went into the kitchen to bring out her homemade cookies that she had baked especially for her. Hot herbal tea accompanied the cookies. Their conversation turned to lighter matters. They talked about starting a project while Laura was recovering; her aunt decided it was time for Laura to learn how to make a quilt. She wanted to hand down the knowledge before she was too old to teach anyone. Her home was decorated with beautiful quilts and pillows she had made over the years. She had supplemented her income by sewing quilts and selling them to the local markets. Laura was excited at the prospect of being taught this valuable tradition.

Eventually, Laura wanted to take a hot shower and go to bed, so her aunt handed her the crutches. On the way, she had to stop and lift the skirt of the crocheted doll. Sure enough, her magical piece of candy lay there waiting for her. She smiled and felt good inside. She felt for the first time in a very long time that everything was going to be all right.

# Chapter 17

LAURA SPENT THE NEXT FEW weeks recovering and learning the art of quilt making. Her aunt paid for her to visit the doctor in the nearby town of Andes, to make sure her ankle was healing properly. Day by day, both Laura's ankle and her emotional outlook on life grew stronger. Her aunt shared with her facts about life that her mother had neglected to teach her. Many of the lessons she learned from her aunt would have made her better equipped to deal with life than she had been when she set out at the tender age of sixteen.

Gracie also tried to explain to Laura the secret to happiness. Laura once believed it was being married to a handsome man and having the money to live comfortably. But after she realized she couldn't have a child with Jim, her perspective of what happiness had changed. Her aunt explained to her that happiness comes from sharing love with someone and giving of yourself, not from what others can give to you. She said, "If you don't feel like you are needed by the people you love, then there will be something important missing in your life. That unconditional exchange of love can never be taken away from you, money or no money, whether you live in a cabin or a mansion."

Over the weeks, Laura healed in many ways as her aunt helped her to discover that she was someone important and special and that she could be happy again—very happy. She'd established a life for herself once, and she knew now that she could do it again. Instead of concentrating on the negatives of the past, she chose to allow the ordeals to strengthen her and to look forward to the challenges of the future. Exposed to these new values, it was as if she had peeled away an old layer of skin and exposed a new vibrancy in herself that she didn't even know existed. She had survived and been strengthened, and she felt this was a sign of things to come for her.

Meanwhile, the time approached for her cast to be removed. She was days away from finishing her first quilt. Her aunt had worked patiently by her side, describing each step that was to follow, guiding Laura through the process of putting together the pieces to create a beautiful and intricate pattern. Laura was astounded that she could create something so amazing. It felt natural to be learning this trade from her aunt, like it was a part of her destiny for this art to be handed down to her. Her mind memorized each step and soaked up the information like a dry sponge. Suddenly, an idea popped into her mind. It was so explosive that it felt like the cork of a champagne bottle had just popped in her head. The words started pouring out as quickly as the foam bubbles pour out of a bottle after the cork has been removed.

"Aunt Gracie!" she exclaimed excitedly. "I just had a wonderful idea."

"What is it, child? What has got you in such an uproar?"

"Well, you know how you told me that I have to find something to do in my life that has meaning for me? Something I can feel good about doing and that will give me a reason for waking up in the morning, not just a job that I have to go to?"

"Yes, dear, I do."

"Well, I think the answer has come to me. I think I know what I want to do with my life."

"That's wonderful, Laura! Please share it with me, by all means."

"Remember I told you that I went back to school a few months ago and started taking college classes in accounting? Well, doesn't running your own business use accounting skills?"

"Why, I do believe it does," Gracie responded hesitantly.

"How about if I open my own business?" Laura said, barely able to contain her excitement. "We can make and sell quilts and other craft items. These quilts alone are probably worth a hundred dollars. You've been selling them to other people for years, and they have been making a profit. Together, we can make enough quilts to sell in my shop. I can live anywhere, and you can live here and mail them to me. I will pay you more for them than I bet you are getting from anyone local." Laura bubbled with excitement.

"I don't know, sweetheart. How will you get the money to open a store?" her aunt inquired.

"Got that figured out too," Laura answered with a childlike grin. "If I get a place in a small town, I can sell my car and use that money to secure a small business loan. I also intend to sell my engagement diamond and wedding band. Then maybe I can rent one of those shops that has an apartment above it and live in the same place I work. It would be perfect."

"It sure sounds like you have a good plan," her aunt answered with resignation. "But don't be too hasty about all of this. Let's do some research and talk to a few people. I have some contacts in the area, and I can introduce you to them."

The next few days before her appointment to have her cast removed, Laura could think of nothing else but her newly acquired plan to start her own business. She spent hours planning on paper what type of inventory she would like to have in her shop, figuring how much it would cost in utilities and rent and other expenses. Gracie finally had to drag her out to the car because it was time for her appointment.

The doctor removed the cast and remarked that Laura's ankle should be as strong as ever once the muscles got in condition after their long period of inactivity. He recommended a few sessions of physical therapy, but Laura knew she didn't have the patience to attend them. She would be back to normal in twice the time of an average person.

On the way home from the appointment, Laura was as excited as ever about working out the details of her future business.

"Laura," her aunt began on the drive back from the doctor, "I have a surprise for you, dear."

Laura was concentrating on the sensation of being able to rotate her ankle without the cast.

"You don't need to give me any surprises," Laura chided. "You've given me a love for life that I never knew I had. How can you give me anything more valuable than that?"

"There is a little somethin' I have tucked away—somethin' that if I don't use now won't be any good to me later, when I'm gone," Gracie explained. "I don't have any children but you, dear. I was never blessed enough to have one of my own. I know in my heart that this is the right time to give this to you."

She looked over at Laura, her eyes wet with emotion. Laura wished they had not been in the car at that moment so she could hold her aunt's hand and concentrate on the specialness of the moment.

"Over the years, I have been puttin' money into a savings account. Living alone, I haven't needed much. My happiness has come from my memories, from the few friends that I have, and from hopin' someday I would be together with you again. Now there is a purpose for that money, Laura—somethin' that can bring shared happiness to both of us. I want you to take that money, Laura, and start your business. I'll be very happy to see you fulfill your dream and know that I was a part of it."

Tears filled Laura's eyes. She couldn't believe that after all this woman had given her, she still had more to give. It was if she was a guardian angel placed on this earth to guide Laura in a time she needed guiding the most. This gesture meant more to her than any gift she had ever received in her entire life. But she felt so guilty, taking the nest egg her aunt had spent years building.

"What if you need that money someday? How can I take something you have spent a lifetime saving?" Laura asked with concern.

"Hopefully, if I ever do need money, you will have made your fortune by then, and then you can take care of me," her aunt said with a smile. "I have faith in you, dear girl. You are a survivor. If you put your mind to it, this business will be a success."

Laura felt the weight of the world lift off her shoulders. She now had a dream, a plan to achieve that dream, and the financial means to get it all started.

Within a week, Laura was walking without a limp. She had been busy taking trips to the nearest bookstore and buying every book she could get her hands on that related to starting a small business. She bought maps and went to the library and did research on the areas she felt were growing and would support her type of business. She was introduced to her aunt's friends, who encouraged her and gave her ideas on the types of crafts that were most popular at the moment. Her next step was to travel to the towns she had narrowed down as prospects and get a feel for how she liked them. She wanted a town that was not too big, not too small, and that attracted tourists but still offered some culture and variety. She also knew that she wanted to stay near the mountains and be within a few hours of her aunt. The mountains were her home, a part of her so ingrained that looking at them was as much a part of her as breathing or talking.

She'd decided that her aunt should be part of the decision-making process, so the two of them packed up the car and hit the road to seek the town destined to hold Laura's future. They traveled the route Laura had mapped out in advance, staying in hotels and quaint bed and breakfasts. They ate lunch in small roadside cafés and visited every craft and antique shop they passed to get ideas for her own shop. They talked to people who lived in the towns and asked if they thought a craft shop would make a nice addition to the community and listened to their ideas about locations. Almost everyone they asked had some sort of opinion and sometimes volunteered more advice than either cared to listen to. On those occasions, Laura and Gracie worked out a routine; Gracie would feign a spell and tell Laura that she had a touch of the vapors and needed to get back to the car and sit down for a bit. Laura would help her back to the car. Each time they broke out in fits of laughter, like two giddy schoolgirls.

Finally, all the locations having been visited, the two women returned to the solitude and peacefulness of Gracie's little log cabin. Laura felt that it was a happy occasion, as well as a sad one. While Laura knew Gracie never wanted to leave her log cabin, she had talked a lot about one town in particular. Gracie and her husband had driven there on many special occasions; Laura could tell she had a fondness for the town of Boone. After thinking about all the possibilities, Laura finally decided that Boone was where she would start her new life. It was located only an hour and a half from Rimrock, so she and Gracie could visit whenever they wanted. Boone offered a variety of cultures and had many tourists throughout the year: the skiing crowd in the winter, and in the summer months it hosted rafters, hikers, gem miners, and other types of summer mountain visitors. She knew as soon as she drove through Boone that it was the place she wanted to call home. She felt comfortable and safe there, and it had her aunt's seal of approval. The next step in her scheme was to establish a base camp to search for the right piece of real estate to make her home and start her business.

Packing up and leaving her aunt with a flurry of mixed emotions, she promised that she would return as soon as she had purchased her new place and take Gracie to see it. She also made her aunt promise to look into getting a telephone. Gracie had never had a reason to have one in the past, but now that she had Laura living a good distance away and wanted to be able to communicate with her on a regular basis, she agreed to try to have one hooked up. Now that her aunt was getting on in years, Laura would also feel better knowing that she had a phone in case of any emergencies.

# Chapter 18

SIX MONTHS LATER, LAURA TURNED the sign on the door to her shop from OPEN to CLOSED. A beautifully hand-painted wooden sign hung outside the door, swaying gently in the afternoon breeze. A band of flowers and ivy circled the name of her shop: PETALS AND QUILTS. She leaned against the door and sighed contentedly. It was five o'clock, and she was closing the doors on another successful day. Her day was not finished, however, because one of her last remaining quilts had been bought that afternoon, and she needed to get to work finishing the ones she had recently started. She also needed to call her aunt to see if she had finished any that she could send to replenish the dwindling stock. Laura breathed in the country-spice scent of the new candles she had ordered. She always made sure she had a scented candle burning so that when people walked into the shop, they would be bombarded not only by the visual beauty of her shop but by pleasant scents as well. It was very rare that a customer would enter her shop and leave without some purchase: a small wreath of dried or silk flowers, some scented candles, or, better yet, one of her increasingly popular quilts. They had been selling like wildfire, and Laura was pleased beyond her greatest expectations.

She locked the door and walked to the back staircase that led upstairs to her apartment. Having missed lunch because of the crowd this afternoon, Laura decided she was hungry for pizza. It was easy enough to have it delivered, and she could get to work on the quilts without having to cook for herself. She went to the small but adequate kitchen and retrieved her purse, which had been lying on the counter. She dug through the bill compartment to take inventory of her money, checking that she had enough for the pizza without having to unlock the register. Lying beside the ten-dollar bill was a business card that kept falling out of her wallet. Feeling that it was important, she kept sticking it in her bill compartment to look at later. Now she remembered it and took the time to turn it over and read it. The name on the front shocked her memory. NICHOLAS JACKSON, DVM.

She had thought about Nick a lot over the past few months. She had been extremely busy, pouring hours of work into each day to get her business started, and she hadn't had the time to contact him. Something else had also been holding her back. She hadn't felt she was ready to begin another relationship. She knew that the sparks that had been ignited between the two of them would be quickly fanned if she contacted him again. She didn't think it was fair to reconnect with him until she had healed the wounds from her first marriage and gotten back on her own two feet. There was also Ester. She had honored Ester's wishes by leaving when she was asked, and she had steered clear of Nick for a good length of time. Surely by now, the two of them would either have strengthened their bond or separated. Laura felt guilty that she hoped the latter had happened.

*Maybe it's time.* She was established in a new place and had her act together. Her heart was definitely on its way to being healed. She was experiencing a sense of peace and well-being that she had never felt at any other time in her life. She attributed it all to having relied on herself to build her new life, using her own strength and skills to make herself successful and independent. Laura looked back and realized that if she had stayed married to Jim, she would have always been a puppet, a passenger, relying on him for everything and having to respond whenever he pulled the strings. She loved her independence and the feeling of self-worth she had established. It almost made her think twice about contacting Nick, for fear of developing any need for anyone who might jeopardize her newfound sense of self-reliance.

*Don't get ahead of yourself, Laura,* she told herself. *You don't even know if he is available.*

She told herself that, first of all, he might be married to Ester. And if he wasn't, he may have found someone else. Third, he might be so angry that she had left without saying good-bye that he wouldn't want to ever talk to her again. She decided that instead of calling him, she would get the address of his business and write him a letter. She felt better about that decision; if he didn't care to respond to her, that would be easier to take than if she called him and had to face rejection over the phone.

A week passed after Laura mailed her letter to Nick that explained where she had been for the past year and why she had left without saying good-bye. She didn't want to get Ester in trouble if they were still together, so she simply explained that Ester didn't want to inconvenience him that day because of the horse that needed attention. Ester and she had decided it was better if Laura took the bus back to her car. She apologized for not giving him a proper thank-you or good-bye. She mentioned that she had thought of him often over the past year and that she was still very grateful for all he had done for her.

Once she calculated when his response might arrive, she waited eagerly for a letter. Every day, she checked the mail as soon as it was delivered. A week turned into two, and then two and a half became three. Laura interpreted the silence to mean that Nick had decided against responding to her. That meant that either he was angry with her or he was attached to someone else. She chastised herself for being upset about his lack of response. After all, Nick was a person she had only met over the course of a few days, and she was the one who'd allowed over a year to pass without getting in touch with him. Still, she felt a sense of loss that Nick wouldn't even respond to her as a friend, as someone who shared a very important time in her life.

This was not the first time in her life she had been disappointed by a man. She eventually gave up searching the mail the moment it arrived. She fell back into her normal routine of attending to the store, and she got on with her life.

Laura decided it was time to expand the social aspect of her life. She made plans to attend a party being thrown by the local Chamber of Commerce. She felt sure she would meet some up-and-coming people her own age. The cocktail party would start at seven, so she planned to close the shop precisely at five so she would have a couple of hours to get ready. At a quarter to five, the bell attached to her door jingled to let her know a customer was entering the store. She had every intention of letting the customer know she was closing in fifteen minutes.

From her spot behind the register, she called out in a pleasant tone,

"Thank you for stopping in, but I have to close up tonight by five. Let me know if you need any assistance. I'll be happy to help you."

The customer was inspecting the candle aisle, his back turned toward her. He didn't turn to acknowledge her comment. Laura felt a bit perturbed that he did not give any indication that he had heard her. She decided to get a closer look at the person. Perhaps she should be alarmed at his furtiveness. Boone had a very low crime rate, but she still felt a bit concerned about being alone at closing time with several hundred dollars in cash on hand.

Pretending to check on merchandise in the wooden-crafts section in the aisle across from the candles, Laura nonchalantly moved into a direct view of the customer. His back was still turned, and she could not get a good look at his face. He was tall, and she could tell that he was rather muscular beneath his heavy jacket. The hair had a familiar style to it, rather on the long side, sort of unkempt-looking, but not at all unattractive. Finally, curiosity got the best of her. She walked directly up to the back of the man and tapped him on the shoulder. This was her store, and she was not going remain apprehensive about this stranger.

"Excuse me, sir."

The man wheeled around and grabbed her, pulling her close, and then kissed her firmly on the mouth. Laura froze with shock and surprise. She pulled away and stared in disbelief.

"Nick!" Laura exclaimed with delight. She threw her arms around his neck and squeezed him as tightly as she could. She couldn't believe he was really there, standing in her store, hugging her back.

"I thought you were angry at me for leaving the way I did," she said, still wrapped in his arms. "When I didn't hear from you, I thought I was never going to see you again."

"Shhhhhhh," he returned softly, stroking the back of her hair with his large, muscular hands. "I just want to hold you for a second so I can cherish this moment. I've been dreaming about it for over a year now, you know."

"You have?" Laura asked, pulling back a bit so she could look into his eyes. "What about Ester? Is she okay?"

Nick explained that he understood Ester's feelings and he'd known all along that she was responsible for Laura leaving without saying good-bye. He explained that she was totally out of his life now. He had arranged for her to work with another vet in a nearby town. In return, the vet's younger brother, fresh out of vet school, was delighted to come and work with Nick. This gave Nick some freedom from being on call twenty-four hours a day.

"I hope you don't mind my surprise visit. I have been planning this since the day I got your letter over two weeks ago, but this was the first opportunity I had to get away," Nick said, already sensing that she was as happy as he to see her.

"Mind? Are you crazy? You coming here tonight is like a wish granted by a fairy godmother. In fact, Prince Charming, I have a party to go to this evening. It just so happens I need a date. If it is not too forward of me to ask, will you be my date?" she asked coyly.

"Why, yes, I would be delighted, even though I am unaccustomed to being solicited for dates by women. Being the southern gentleman that I am, I am usually the one that does the asking."

"I guess that will teach you to show up unannounced at a lady's doorstep," she countered. "Now, if you will allow me to lock my door, we can commence with socializing," Laura said. She took his hand and led him to the front door. It was five o'clock on the dot when she bolted the door and led Nick through the back of the store and up the back stairs to see her apartment.

# Chapter 19

LAURA WAS CAREFUL TO TAKE the courtship process more slowly than she had with Jim. She felt like she knew Nick better than she ever did Jim, right off the bat. Going through several crisis situations with Nick allowed her to see the type of person he really was, rather than just a façade, as Jim had given. He listened to her with quiet understanding when she told him about her past, and he not only accepted who she had been but thought more of her for what she had become. He even admitted finally that he was glad that time had passed between when they first met and when they actually started dating. It proved that what they had was real because it passed the first test, the test of time.

Because of Laura's business, she was not able to take time off to go and visit Nick, but Nick's partner allowed him to take every other weekend off to visit her. He would hang out on Saturdays until the shop closed, and then they had Saturday evening and all of Sunday on their own. After a few months of dating, Laura even gave him the real test, bringing him home to meet Aunt Gracie, who loved him immediately. Gracie felt like she knew him already from all the glowing reports Laura had given her.

There was an unspoken uneasiness about making their lives together more permanent because each of them had a thriving business in different towns. Laura would often change the subject when Nick hinted about proposing to her. She loved Nick dearly and recognized all the signs Aunt Gracie had shared about finding one's soul mate. She believed he was a person she could be happy with forever. But the needy woman inside her was gone, and in her place was an independent person who was afraid of the pain of needing someone. Another aspect of their relationship also frightened her. The issue finally emerged while Nick and Laura were together on Valentine's Day evening.

They were sharing one of their treasured Saturday nights. Often, Laura would cook for Nick, and they would be content spending hours at her apartment talking and watching movies, at peace with one another's company. But Nick insisted that he wanted to take Laura to a nice restaurant for dinner for Valentine's.

He arranged to have a florist deliver a dozen of the most beautiful white roses Laura had ever seen. He told her that instead of the traditional red, he had chosen white to symbolize the pureness of his love for her. The thought touched her, and she knew the evening was going to be special.

A year and a half had passed since they started dating. Nick had been hinting lately that he could not stand the two-week breaks between seeing her. She felt that Nick was coming to a point in their relationship where he needed more from her. But something was holding her back from wanting to accept that things had to change. She returned Nick's love in every way, but something deep inside of her remained fearful of moving on from where they were. Laura could not define what that fear was and thought maybe it was a residual fear of marriage caused by the pain from her divorce. The horrible memories from that experience still haunted her.

Nick made reservations at the most posh and romantic restaurant in town. Laura bought a new dress, a bright red strapless taffeta gown, tea-length. The lines of the dress were simple yet elegant, and she felt like royalty when Nick inspected her with extreme approval. They drove to the restaurant and were seated immediately in a corner table for two with a white lace tablecloth and a single red rose centerpiece. A candle flickered, dance-like, to the soft music playing in the background. Nick ordered a bottle of wine, and he held her hand across the table as they engaged in quiet conversation.

"You are so beautiful, Laura," Nick said with admiration.

Laura blushed slightly and looked down at the table, her soft brown hair forming waves around her face. Embarrassed by his compliments, she felt her cheeks flush, but she loved the warm feeling he gave her.

Then he added, "I want you to have a daughter who is as beautiful as you are."

Stunned, Laura looked at Nick intently. She had told Nick bits and pieces of her desire to have children and the disaster that had occurred because of it during her first marriage.

"I mean it, Laura. You were meant to have gorgeous babies, and you are going to make some lucky child the most wonderful mother in the world."

Tears filler her eyes no matter how hard she tried to hold them back. The memories came flooding back like a giant wave, memories of how she felt holding her neighbor's baby and the love and maternal instincts she had developed, even for her dog.

Nick reached over and wiped the tears from her eyes, but she could not respond to Nick's statement. She found it hard to breathe.

"I know how much you want a family, Laura, and I think I know you love me. I know I love you more than I have ever loved anyone in my entire life. From the moment I first saw you, disheveled and abandoned on the side of the road, you were special to me. And when you magically appeared in my life a second time, I took it as a sign from heaven that we were destined to be together. I waited for you for a whole year. When your letter came to me, it was if I had been waiting my whole life for that one piece of mail."

Then Nick let go of Laura's hand and reached into his pocket. He pulled out a crumpled letter, the first one Laura had sent him. Still unable to speak, Laura managed a smile through her tears, a smile that melted Nick's heart. He placed the letter on the table between them so Laura would understand the significance of what he was about to ask her.

Reaching for her hand again, Nick continued. "I want to be a part of your family, your life. I want to be the father of your children. I can no longer live my life apart from you, waiting weeks at a time to hold you and be with you. I want to wake up every morning beside you, your face the last thing I see before I go to sleep and the first thing I see every morning when I open my eyes. I want to have the pleasure of your warmth beside me every night when I fall asleep."

Nick picked up her soft, trembling hand and pressed it to his lips. The tears still trickled down her face. He knew that there was uneasiness about her, like a frightened mare about to bolt, but he continued anyway.

"I love you with all my heart. Laura, will you be my wife? Will you marry me?"

A smile passed through her like the whisper of a breeze, and then she looked down again. She couldn't understand why she felt so strange. She'd known this proposal was coming; maybe she hadn't known it would be tonight, but she knew it was inevitable. Why did she feel so unprepared to give Nick an answer? Why did she feel so frightened?

Laura did not respond immediately. She furrowed her brow and looked down at the table.

"Are you all right?" he asked.

"Yes, I'm fine," she sniffed, and she wiped her eyes and nose on the napkin. "I just don't know what to say." Her voice was shaky.

"Say yes and make me the happiest man on earth," Nick said, leaning forward and trying to get Laura to meet his gaze. "I don't have a ring yet because I did this spontaneously. It just felt right."

"The ring doesn't matter. And my hesitation is not because I don't love you. I guess I wasn't prepared for this. I'm caught a little off guard. It is such a monumental decision," she replied, trying to smooth over her indecisive feelings.

"I understand," Nick said, even though he felt a little let down that she did not reply with an immediate yes.

"I'll tell you what. I'm going home tomorrow. Why don't you take the next two weeks and think about it. Is that enough time? Am I pressuring you too much?" he asked with genuine concern.

"You are the most sensitive, wonderful man on earth. Thank you for understanding that I need some time to think about a few things," she offered, hoping that she had not offended this wonderful man, whom she loved with all her heart.

"As long as you promise me that taking time to think about my proposal is not an indication that you are leaning toward saying no," he added, trying to lighten her mood.

"Of course not," she managed to say in a more lighthearted manner. "It is just that I am an independent woman now, and I need time to think about some of the changes that my life will go through if I say yes."

"When you say yes, you mean," Nick added hopefully.

"How can I resist your charm and handsome face? And you have offered me a bribe that you know means more to me than anything in the world. You want to be the father of my children."

"Then what is there to think about?" Nick asked, still hoping for a yes so he would not have to wait for two long weeks.

"Ah, you promised me some time. I don't know if I can marry a man who forgets so quickly those things he so recently promised," she kidded with him.

"Okay, okay, no more talk tonight on the subject, even though my every thought will be of nothing else for two weeks. Talk about torture."

The evening unfolded into a night of romance. Both were saddened when the next day arrived and Nick once again had to return to his life far away from Laura.

Laura had two weeks to give Nick her answer. She had promised him an answer, and she would die rather than break that promise. She was just so afraid of revealing her past to Nick and telling him that she was responsible for the death of her father. Right now, she had a wonderful relationship with the man she loved, and there were no strings attached. If she agreed to marry Nick and did not tell him the truth about her past, it was the same as lying to him. She'd learned from her first marriage how important knowing the truth about the other person was; she just didn't know how to tell Nick. What if he didn't want her anymore after finding out the truth? She decided she had stalled long enough; now she had some decisions to make.

After Nick had proposed to her, she was in turmoil. She couldn't concentrate on what she was supposed to be doing, and she certainly wasn't in any mood to deal with customers. One day on her way back from having lunch down the street from her shop, she passed the travel agency. A poster on the window advertised a five-day getaway package to the Cayman Islands. The poster depicted a gorgeous beach at sunset and a woman in a bikini reclining on the sand without a towel, resting on her elbows. Her head was tilted back, allowing the last rays of sunshine to wash across her body. The ocean was a mesmerizing crystal blue. She was alone with the pristine sand and the gently rolling waves, miles of clean, white sand winding its way into the horizon. Laura stood transfixed, staring at the image and picturing herself lying on that beach. She had a brief thought that she could have been that girl on the beach had things worked out with Jim, but she knew in her heart that she would trade that fantasy in an instant to make everything right with Nick.

# Chapter 20

ONE OF LAURA'S BIGGEST FEARS was that someone from her past would surface and the questions about her disappearance would begin. She thought long and hard about how to make things right and what the chances were of that really happening. So many years had passed that she doubted anyone would even remember the incident, but still, what if she was wrong? It would be terrible for Nick to have his future wife under investigation. She pictured a scenario where their engagement announcement made the paper and someone recognized her name. She was sure that there were still people around the police force who were part of the team that searched for her. She put her hands on her head and shook with frustration. She didn't have a clue what to do or how to go about finding the answers that she needed. Maybe it was time to call Aunt Gracie. It was a starting point; perhaps she would have some insight on how to help. All Laura knew for sure was that she had to get this part of her life resolved before she could face Nick and tell him the truth. She had to be a hundred percent sure she was not bringing unwanted chaos into his life because she had not been able to face her past.

The first week flew by. Nick and Laura talked on the phone several times, and Laura was careful to keep the conversations short and limited to their daily activities. Then the weekend arrived. Laura closed the shop on Sunday and posted the CLOSED sign on her door. She had to make a trip to Rimrock and set things right. She hated to lose the business, but she knew it was important and had to be done. Earlier, Laura had called her aunt and told her she was coming to visit on Sunday. Laura told Gracie that she needed her advice on an important issue, and Gracie had accepted that answer without pressing Laura.

Laura got into her BMW and began the hour-and-a-half drive to her aunt's house. Laura had promised to call Nick on Saturday, but she had not, and he had not called her, as he was trying to give her space. She was sure he would be worried about not hearing from her, so she decided to put on her earpiece and talk to him during her drive.

Nick picked up on the second ring.

"Laura. Why didn't you call yesterday?" he asked with concern.

"I'm sorry, I was busy all day yesterday. I haven't even had time to breathe let alone make a phone call. But I do miss you."

"I miss you too. Maybe you didn't call because you wanted to surprise me that you have some good news for me a week early?" Nick asked hopefully, a touch of humor in his voice.

"Actually, I am on my way up to spend the day with my aunt. I needed to get away from the shop so I could do some thinking. You know that I didn't think through some of my past decisions very well. I just want to make sure I am doing the right thing this time. At least I want to make sure I've thought everything through. "

"But sometimes you can think too much. If you overanalyze everything, you can make yourself paranoid with all the potential problems you might encounter. Sometimes you just have to follow your heart, Laura," Nick entreated. "I don't think there is a person in this world who has made a wrong decision when they have truly followed their heart's desire."

Laura thought a moment. "That is easy to say when you haven't had your heart broken and been dumped on the street with just the clothes on your back."

"Stop right there, young lady," Nick interrupted. "I don't want to hear that for an excuse anymore. I have had my share of heartaches too, you know. This is about me and you, not about what happened between you and anyone else. I love you, and I would never hurt you. What this boils down to is do you love and trust me? That is the decision that you have to think about. Don't put me in a category with anyone else."

"I guess I never thought about it that way," Laura admitted.

"Oh, great. You have to torture me for two weeks and hear this revelation over the phone in order for it to sink in?" Nick chided.

"Don't get too wrapped up in your psychological evaluation. I still have some things to work out in my own mind that don't have anything to do with you. Not only that, but I have to deal with the fact that we are going to have to make some big adjustments in our lives, and you know it. I worked very hard to start my own business, and you have a successful practice where you are. Unless we are going to be a married couple living in separate parts of the state, one of us is going to have to give something up. My guess is that it will have to be me."

"Is that what's bothering you? Laura, I will do whatever it takes to make you happy. Don't you know that about me yet? I love you so much I would move to Alaska for you."

"I don't necessarily know if it is fair to ask either one of us to give up what we have. People need you, Nick. You have spent years developing a practice. And my business has healed me from the inside. It has made me feel like a success for the first time in my life. I'm just so torn ..." Laura couldn't finish the sentence and suddenly choked up with emotion. She hadn't intended for the conversation to turn this serious. She just wanted to call him and let him know she was taking a day trip; now she was all upset.

"All right, please don't upset yourself. We will work something out. I promise. I also promise that if you agree to marry me, you will be so happy starting our lives together and raising a family that all this will seem trivial."

"I have to go now, "Laura said, trying to compose herself.

"Laura," Nick pleaded, "please listen to your heart. You know we love each other. Everything will work out if you just give it a chance. And please drive carefully. I hate that you are driving when you are so upset."

"I'll be fine," she managed to say. "I really have to go now. I love you, bye."

Half an hour later, Laura made the exit off the four-lane highway onto the two-lane road that wound its way up the mountainside. The change forced Laura to pay attention to her driving again. She had drifted off, deep in thought about what this day had in store for her. She just wanted her life to go smoothly for once, to be able to fall in love and marry the most wonderful man she had ever met. She resented the fact that she had to put herself through this torture just to rid the demons from her past. She was frustrated that things had been going so well for her, and now it seemed like she was taking one giant step back. She knew she had to do this in order to move forward with her life. Dealing with her past was like a festering splinter that had to be removed before healing could take place.

It was painful but necessary. The worst part for her was having to involve people she loved, like Aunt Gracie and Nick. Part of making everything right was telling them the truth, and she hated letting down the only two people in her life she loved and cared about.

The S-curves in the road forced her to slow down and concentrate, but the steep grade of the hill was no match for her car's powerful engine. She pressed down on the gas pedal, accelerating into the sharp turns. The car handled smoothly, and she drove on, confident that she was in total control. Laura's knuckles turned white as she gripped the steering wheel and continued the ascent. She just wanted to get this day over with. The steep grade began to even out at the top of the mountain, and Laura began to relax her grip on the wheel. She was easing off the gas pedal when suddenly a deer jumped into the road in front of her. Laura did not see it coming, and she immediately swerved to her right to avoid hitting it. Her reactions were so quick that she didn't have time to stop herself from oversteering. The sleek black car raced toward the hillside, and Laura didn't have time to react before it collided with the trees. Laura's body flew forward as the car collided with the trees, and the airbags exploded to life. Her body slammed the airbag, which softened the impact, but the car tipped over sideways into the small ravine next to the row of trees. Laura's head crashed into the driver's-side window as the car rolled over. Her world went dark.

Laura's eyes were shut, but she could sense the space around her. She was lying in an uncomfortable position, her neck bent sideways and her body crumpled against the driver's-side door. Her head exploded with pain, too much to try to force herself back to complete consciousness. Her breathing was slow and rhythmic, and her body felt weightless, detached from her pain. She felt a part of herself leave and float a few inches above her body. She knew there was something she had to see—something she had to remember. In an instant, she found herself outside the shack where she grew up, just an observer. She saw a young girl, a thin sixteen-year-old in a pale nightgown and robe, standing barefoot with a pack of matches in her hand. She looked cold and scared but very determined. The father, standing on the porch, bellowed in a drunken slur for the girl to get her ass back in the house. He gripped the porch pole and threatened to come out and get her if she didn't come back immediately. The man, in the darkness of the night, did not see the trembling hands of the sixteen-year-old as she struggled with a match to ignite a flame. The girl finally got the match to light. Laura's breaths quickened; she knew what was going to happen next. But she struggled to remain detached, captivated as the events unfolded.

The girl looked briefly at the flaming match in her hand and again at the man staggering in the doorway. She made her decision and tossed the match onto the ground in front of her. A small snake of light began to form and race its way toward the cabin. She watched the drunken man in the doorway, who had just noticed the smell of gasoline in the air, his senses dulled from the alcohol. She thought that he looked confused as he saw a path of light moving quickly toward him, and she watched him step back and stagger as he noticed the gas can and the wet puddle beneath his feet. She noted that as he looked up again, he saw the light climbing the stairs, quickly approaching. He tried to react, but there was an explosion of light, an intense and searing heat. The girl gasped as she watched him fall back through the doorway into the cabin, a brightly burning mass of flames. The dry, poorly built shack quickly fueled the fire. The front of the shack became enveloped in the hungry flames. The girl stepped back a bit from the intensity of the flames and used her arms to shield her face from the searing heat. The heat warmed her cold, shivering body. Laura knew she felt a great sense sadness but also relief that it was all over. She was still scared and shaking, but for the first time in her life, she had control. She was finally getting revenge for the atrocities that had plagued her entire life. The pain, the torture, would finally stop.

Time went by, but Laura was unaware of how much. She drifted in and out of consciousness. She barely remembered being pried out of the car and lifted onto a stretcher. Flashing lights hurt her eye, and she pressed them tightly closed to keep out the biting light. People spoke to her, but she stayed in her shell and shut their voices out. She felt the stretcher lift and settle in the back of the ambulance and someone place a warm blanket over her body. Someone else put an ice pack on the side of her head. Nausea was creeping its way into her senses, and she fought to stay in the soothing blackness. It was easy for her to give way to the nothingness.

# Chapter 21

By the following day, Laura was awake and feeling much better. She had suffered a concussion, but the doctors said that all her vital signs were good, and she was ready to be released. They had done a CAT scan and felt confident that with a week's rest, she would be fine. They gave her a list of possible symptoms to watch for and told her to come back to the hospital immediately if any of them occurred.

Gracie had come immediately when she heard about the accident. They had looked on Laura's cell phone and seen Gracie's number as an emergency contact. Laura could tell she was devastated by Laura's accident and worried sick about her, but Laura assured her that she would be fine. Her car, on the other hand, was totaled, and that was going to be more of an issue. She felt sick knowing she had wrecked the expensive car.

As Gracie waited for her to change from the hospital gown back into her street clothes, the nurse came into Laura's room.

"There is a policeman here to see Laura. Is she dressed and ready for company?"

Just then, Laura came out of the bathroom, dressed to leave. A uniformed officer stood in the doorway to her room. He approached Laura and asked her to sit down so he could ask her a couple of questions about the accident.

Laura's heart raced in her chest. She felt her stomach squeeze into a tight knot. She sat on the bed and tried to control her breathing.

The officer stared at her and asked her, "Are you okay, ma'am?"

"I'm fine. I'm okay. Let's just get this over with so I can go home. My head still really hurts."

"I just need to ask you a few questions, since we were not able to ask you at the scene of the accident."

The officer asked her to give the details of the accident. Laura explained that the deer had jumped in front of her and she had swerved to avoid it. The officer asked her questions about her speed, if she had been using a cell phone, and if she had consumed any alcohol. Laura answered all the questions to his satisfaction, and he wrote the answers down on his report.

"There is one more thing I need to ask you. You are Laura Atwood from Rimrock, correct?"

Laura went white as a sheet. Because she had changed back to her maiden name after the divorce, her name had now sent up a red flag. She felt like she was suffocating and took in a deep, rasping breath. The policeman looked at her and gave her a moment to compose herself and then repeated the question.

"Yes, I am."

She looked down at her hands, which were clenched in her lap, and waited for the next question she knew he would ask.

"When your name came up on our police report, it indicated you were flagged for being a missing person some years back. What happened to you?"

Laura was so taken aback by being confronted that she didn't know what to say. She simply gave the answer that when her home caught fire, she'd escaped and her parents hadn't. She said she was so upset she just ran away. She told the policeman that she'd stayed in shelters and eventually got a job and became self-sufficient. Gracie stood next to her with her hand on her shoulder and nodded as Laura revealed her story.

Aunt Gracie then explained who she was and confirmed that Laura had disappeared out of her life as well. But she was back now, and everything had worked itself out.

"Well, then, I guess I can take you off the missing persons list. Sorry about your parents, Laura. I am sure that must have been really difficult for you. I'm glad you are okay now. I guess I have everything I need from you."

Laura watched as the policeman turned and walked from her room. With him, he took the fear and apprehension that had been bottled up inside her for so many years. She put her face in her hands and cried. Gracie sat next to her on the bed and cradled her in her arms.

When Laura and Aunt Gracie arrived back at Gracie's cabin, there was a dark blue truck waiting in the driveway. Of course Nick could not stay away. Gracie had called him as soon as she heard about Laura's accident, and he had dropped everything and driven to be with her. Since Laura did not have a car, Nick packed Laura into his truck and drove her back to her store. Laura slept much of the ride back, and when she was awake, they mostly cuddled and drove in silence. Laura was thankful that Nick had come to be with her, and she realized then how much she needed him in her life. Now that she had been cleared for her disappearance and her fears had been alleviated about her past, it was time to have a talk with Nick. He knew most of the story about that night, but she needed to tell him the rest. Telling him scared her to death.

Laura did not have an appetite, but Nick insisted that they stop for a bite to eat before returning to her apartment above her store. It was getting late, and all Laura wanted was an opportunity to talk to Nick and tell him the truth, but they stopped for a quick late dinner at a diner along the highway. An hour later, Nick had tucked Laura under one of the colorful quilts she had made. She snuggled into the feather-top mattress and was thankful to be home, safe. Nick climbed into bed next to her and whispered into her ear how much he loved her. She returned his embrace and smiled, telling him that she was glad he was here and she was not angry with him in the least for showing up uninvited.

*Now is the time*, Laura thought, *before I lose my nerve.* She would tell Nick about what she had done to her father on the night she ran away from home. She explained to Nick that before she could go any further in their relationship, she had to come clean about the details of her past. This was the baggage she had been referring to, and now was the time for her to share it so he could decide if he still wanted to be with her. Nick listened quietly. As she lay in the dark, holding him tightly so he could not see the pain written on her face, she carefully described the events that unfolded, starting with the brutal beating of her mother on that fateful night. She explained that she had watched as her father murdered her mother and that she had barely escaped with her life. Then she described how she tripped over the gas can and the idea came to her to save herself once and for all from her father's torture. Nick listened, without judgment, as Laura described lighting the porch and her father on fire. They both cried as she once again remembered the horror of the evening. She asked Nick if he could ever love a woman who had killed her own father. He replied as he hugged her tightly that she was an angel. She had rid the world of an evil man, and she had acted in self-defense. He promised her that someday they would visit her old home and lay to rest to her mother's memory and come to peace with her past. It was the only way she would truly get over her past and be at peace with her future. And now that she had come to terms with her memory, it was time to move on.

Then, when they were about to fall asleep, wrapped securely in each other's arms, Laura whispered Nick's name.

"Nick, are you asleep?" she whispered softly.

"Ummm ..." he muttered.

"Yes," she whispered.

"What did you say?" Nick asked, suddenly more awake.

"I said yes. I will marry you. You have rescued me for the third time, and I feel that three is a charm. I have to marry you now."

Laura couldn't see Nick's face in the dark, but she knew he was crying silent tears of joy. She felt at peace inside as he hugged her tightly and thanked her for making his life complete. Laura knew in her heart that she had made the right decision. The two of them were meant to be together, forever.

When the morning light arrived, the tired couple slept, blissfully happy, until the noises around town finally woke them. Nick had to make sure that her acceptance of his proposal wasn't a dream. She reaffirmed her decision, and the two of them prepared to celebrate for the entire day. Laura left the closed sign on the door, and Nick prepared to take her shopping in town and let her pick out an engagement ring. Laura was thrilled with the idea of picking out her own diamond ring.

# Chapter 22

LAURA AND NICK'S WEDDING WAS a simple ceremony performed in a quaint, tiny Methodist church nestled back in the woods in Nick's hometown. Nick's parents, a few of his close friends, Aunt Gracie, and a few of Gracie's friends were in attendance. White doves were released by the newlyweds as they exited the church, and then they climbed into the waiting carriage, drawn by two white Percherons. The horses danced and jingled as the newlyweds climbed into the red velvet seats of the shiny white carriage, and then they headed off, clipping and clopping rhythmically down the road through town to the reception hall. The wedding and reception were small, but the love of the bride and groom was clear to all. The celebration itself was immense.

The honeymoon was pleasantly uneventful. Mr. and Mrs. Nicholas Jackson returned from their vacation ready to begin their lives together, with Laura filling the role as Nick's new assistant, secretary, and bookkeeper. Laura adapted quickly to her new position. She discovered that she was good with animals and quickly adapted to being Nick's animal handler, complementing Nick's talent for dealing with his patients.

Six months passed. Laura felt it was right that she had moved to where Nick had spent many years developing his practice. She had found a solution by passing her business to her aunt. After all, her aunt's life savings had brought the business to life. It was the perfect solution to her dilemma. Gracie had been happy and excited that Laura was getting married and eager to help her in any way possible. She would live in the apartment above the store and keep her home as a vacation cabin, a place where she and Laura could get together for holidays. She accepted the management of the store under one condition: that Laura would still come to visit once a month and make sure that Gracie wasn't making a mess of things. She also wanted Laura to keep track of the books, because Gracie didn't feel confident she could handle the accounting end of the business.

Finally, Laura began to feel at home in the small rural town of which she was now a part. She'd never realized all the acquaintances Nick had, and all of them were eager to accept Laura into their close-knit community. The younger women invited her to have lunch with them; the older women baked her pies and casseroles and visited often, bringing a variety of treats. Even the children of the community accepted Laura in her role as the new wife of Dr. Jackson. Laura visited the local elementary school on career day with Nick and loved the attention lavished on her and Nick by all the eager children, who asked questions about what it was like being a veterinarian: the dream job of almost every nine-year-old girl in the school.

After their visit to the school, Laura felt the yearnings of motherhood once again. Nick and she talked that evening about starting a family of their own. They both decided that they would let nature take its course; when the time was right, Laura would conceive her first child. The thought never occurred to either one of them that Laura would have difficulty conceiving. But after two months of trying to get pregnant with no success, Laura began to worry. Both of them went to the doctor to get checked out, but neither showed any signs of infertility. The doctor confirmed that sometimes worrying too much about getting pregnant could cause a couple to have difficulty conceiving and said that they both needed to relax and let nature take its course.

Trying their best to put their concerns to rest, Nick and Laura went on with their daily routines. Fall and early winter eventually arrived at the mountains, and Nick and Laura had more time to spend relaxing in their home, cuddling by the warm fire and watching the white, puffy flakes of snow drift by their picture window. Laura loved winter, and she felt safe, warm, and entirely happy being married to Nick.

Finally, Christmas was a week away. Laura concentrated on making her and Nick's first Christmas together an event to remember the rest of their lives. She spent hours turning their charming home into a showcase fit for the *Better Homes and Gardens* Christmas issue. She made crafts, from cinnamon-scented pinecones to oranges spiked with cloves, to hang around the house. She built elaborate gingerbread homes and even sewed a gorgeous quilt with red and green squares to drape over them when they sat by the fireplace. They had taken a sleigh ride to a Christmas-tree farm and handpicked the biggest tree they thought could fit in their house. They dragged it home and decorated it with white lights, tiny red bows, wooden ornaments, and a shining gold star that Aunt Gracie had sent as an early Christmas gift.

Christmas Eve arrived, and Nick and Laura lay by the fire on a sheepskin rug and drank hot cider after having spent the day caroling through town, as was Nick's custom every year. Laura raised her glass and toasted Nick and told him it was time for her to give him his gift. As the light of the fire illuminated her glistening eyes as they looked into his, Laura announced to Nick that she had indeed experienced the miracle of the season. Her joy and happiness and the love between them had grown so much that she was now carrying a new life, one started by their perfect union, the result of them sharing so much love together that their love had overflowed and ignited a new spirit. Laura was finally carrying the child she had dreamed about for so long.

In all the world, Laura and Nick felt as if that Christmas Eve was more special to them than it could be for any couple on earth. They sat in front of the fire until Christmas morning dawned and shared their hopes and dreams for the new life they'd created. Finally, falling asleep for a few hours, the couple slept under the quilt that Laura had made to celebrate their first Christmas together, and both dreamed of sweet baby breath and tiny little feet pitter-pattering around their home.

The next months flew by. The first few months were not too pleasant for her, when she experienced the nausea and discomfort of her body adjusting to the battering of hormonal changes. Nick took on many of the responsibilities Laura had been doing and insisted that she stay home in bed until she felt better. He played the role of the doting, adoring husband and eager father and brought her cut flowers, pints of exotic flavors of ice cream, books on childbearing, and any other stereotypical pregnant-mother gifts he could get his hands on. Eventually, the nausea want away, and Laura felt the need to get out of the house and return to work. The new experience of watching her flat, firm belly swell, her breasts start to enlarge, and her emotions turn from stoic to weepy all fascinated her. She savored every moment of the growth and development of her unborn child and pleasantly accepted the good feelings as well as the bad.

The couple carefully planned out each detail of their life that needed to be adapted to accommodate their new addition. They decorated a room for the baby and bought all new furniture to add to the décor. They bought a car seat and signed up for natural-childbirth classes. By the time the eighth month arrived, Laura's friends gave Laura her baby shower, and she felt more than ready to have the baby. Every detail had been planned for and attended to, right down to the neatly packed diaper bag of tiny infant outfits. It also included a soft, downy receiving blanket folded and packed with the anticipation of wrapping the precious bundle in it on his first day in the world.

Not realizing that her sudden burst of energy and her urge to clean everything in sight were signs that labor was about to begin, Laura made a project of dragging several heavy braided rugs out onto the porch. She tugged and pulled the rugs over the porch railing and began beating them with a broom to remove the dust and dirt that had accumulated deep within the braids, which a vacuum could not remove. Little by little, she noticed a dull ache in her lower back that she attributed to dragging the rugs, not to labor. She knew Nick would have a fit if he caught her dragging the heavy rugs around, so she wanted to finish the job and replace the rugs before he got back from work.

Eventually, the pains in her back increased and an aching cramp developed in her abdomen. Laura still had one more rug to drag into the house, and even though by then she suspected that labor had begun, she knew that she would probably have several hours or more of contractions before the final stages of labor developed.

Deciding that she would attempt to drag the last rug back in the house herself just to avoid any confrontation with her husband, Laura grasped the rug and pulled it over the porch railing. As she began pulling, an extremely sharp pain shot through her belly. Laura doubled over and felt totally helpless as the pain gripped her unexpectedly. She had been preparing for the pain of labor for weeks, but now that it was actually here, she was surprised at the sudden intensity.

Dropping the rug on the ground, Laura rose to a standing position and began walking slowly toward the door, breathing deeply, both hands wrapped around her protruding belly. Her only goal was to get to her cell phone and call Nick. She knew he would have his cell on and would respond quickly to her call. She reached for the sliding door. As she pulled the heavy door aside, another contraction took hold of her, even more intense than the last one and lasting longer. Laura started to get nervous. The contractions were not supposed to be coming this hard and this close together yet. Standing in the doorway, trying to recover her breath, she suddenly felt a warm gush of liquid roll down her leg. Laura whimpered, knowing that now that her water had broken, the baby could come at any time. She had to get to her phone, attached to a charger on the kitchen counter, and she tried to keep the panic she was feeling from making matters worse. *Things are still under control,* she told herself, using her inner strength to keep herself calm. Still holding her belly tightly, as if that act would keep the baby from slipping any further down the birth canal, she walked through the living room into the kitchen and finally reached the phone. Only a couple of minutes had passed since the last contraction, but as Nick answered the phone on the second ring, another one seized her body.

"Nick," she yelled, sounding on the verge of panic. She was unable to speak for a few seconds because the pain was so intense.

Nick could hear her moaning in the background. "Laura, Laura! Speak to me! Tell me what is going on," Nick implored.

"M-m-m-my water broke, and, oh God, Nick, it hurts so much, and the contractions are coming too quickly. You've got to get me to the hospital!" she managed to gasp before falling into her rhythm of short, shallow breaths.

Nick jumped into his truck and started the engine.

"I'm about twelve miles away, at the Anderson farm. I will be there in ten minutes. Just hang on. Use the breathing we've been practicing. Lie on the couch and try to stay relaxed. And Laura, I love you. You can do this, baby. I'm on my way."

Nick bolted, leaving Mr. Anderson quite bewildered as he watched him drive away like a bat out of hell. Mr. Anderson scratched his head as the pig he held squealed and flailed, and then he finally walked back to the pen to deposit the screaming pig.

Nick immediately phoned their nearest neighbor. Mrs. Lafferty was always volunteering to help in any way possible, and she was delighted when Nick asked her to go and sit with Laura until he arrived. Delightedly, she squealed, "The baby is coming, the baby is coming," and she was already on the way out the door before Nick finished his sentence.

Nick hadn't gotten more than a mile down the road when his phone rang again.

"Laura?" he answered immediately, "What's the matter? Why are you calling again? Is something wrong?"

"Nick, I'm so afraid. I think I feel like pushing," Laura screamed into the phone, obviously panicking now.

"Is Mrs. Lafferty there? She is on her way over."

"She just walked in … Oh, no-o-o-o. Nick, the baby is coming. I … can't … keep …from … *pushing*!" Laura dropped the phone to the floor, screaming in pain.

Nick, hearing her screams, pushed the accelerator to the floor. In less than five minutes he slid into the driveway, almost crashing into Laura's new car. He jumped out of the truck, leaving it running, and almost tripped and fell in his hurry to ascend the front steps. He threw the door open and flew into the living room. He dashed over to the couch, where he saw Laura propped up on pillows. Mrs. Lafferty, a worried look on her face, was watching the head of the baby start to crown.

Nick took over immediately. First he bent over and kissed his wife, who was sweating profusely and crying tears of pain and anxiety. Putting the imminent birth aside, Nick knelt beside her and put his face close to hers.

"Laura, I want you to look at me," Nick directed in a calm voice, although every inch of him was shaking.

She turned her eyes toward him, and in that instant, Nick fell in love with her all over again. He could see the fear and pain in her eyes, but beneath the fear he could see her inner strength. The woman he had married, the one about to bring his child into the world, was a survivor.

"Everything is going to be fine, Laura. I have delivered hundreds of babies, albeit none of them human, but I know the mechanics, sweetheart. Do you trust me?"

Laura only nodded, her face reddening again, her breath held in by the involuntary pushing her body was now doing to force the baby into the world.

"Okay then, let's have this baby, shall we? You never do anything the easy way, Mrs. Jackson, so I guess I will just have to rescue you one more time. Mrs. Lafferty, get as many towels as you can find. I will need my box from the truck with the sterile equipment to cut the cord," he immediately directed, taking his position to deliver the baby.

Mrs. Lafferty, happy to be doing something productive, ran off to get the supplies.

Looking up at Laura, Nick said, "I bet this is the last time she volunteers to help around here."

Laura didn't even hear him. She was thrown into another wave of painful contractions, this time pushing with all her might. Her faced turned the color of a beet as she groaned and strained, her teeth clenched, fingers digging into the pillows beside her.

"You're doing fine, Laura," Nick encouraged her. "The baby's head is coming through. One more big push and I think the head will come out. That is the hardest part, sweetheart. Keep pushing. That's a girl."

Laura took a couple of seconds to gather her strength and take a few deep, cleansing breaths. When the next contraction built up, she gave her most tremendous pushing effort.

Mrs. Lafferty had just returned with the towels and the box from the truck. She was just in time to see the baby's head pop into view, the result of Laura's intense pushing.

"Okay, stop a second, Laura. I need you to listen. I know you are going to feel like pushing again, but the hard part is over. I need to suction the baby's nose and rotate him slightly, and the rest of his body is going to follow easily."

"I want to push again," Laura screamed at him. "I want to push now!"

Nick barked orders at Mrs. Lafferty. Fumbling through his equipment, she quickly pulled out a bag with a bulb and syringe and tore open the package and handed it to Nick. Nick cleared the baby's nose and mouth and rotated the baby's head gently to the side to allow the shoulders to easily pass through behind the head.

Laura could no longer stand the pain and started pushing again involuntarily.

"Okay, baby, here we go." Nick had just finished the rotation when Laura gave one final, tremendous push.

The body of the baby slid quickly through the passage, and Nick caught the tiny, white-coated body in his large hands. Laura sat back, exhausted, breathing heavily, and Nick stared unbelievingly at the new life he held in his hands. The baby stretched and whimpered and let out a small cry, filling his new lungs with air.

Mrs. Lafferty looked over and watched the special moment as Nick announced to his wife that they had just delivered their baby boy. Holding the baby up, careful of the umbilical cord, Nick grabbed a towel from Mrs. Lafferty, wrapped the baby gently, and passed the baby to Laura, who instantly cradled him to her chest. Tears of joy and relief rolled down her cheeks as she kissed the baby's perfect little head, crowned with a layer of dark, matted hair. She smiled at Nick as he reached up and wiped her brow with a dry cloth and told her that he loved her and their new baby boy and what a tremendous job she had done.

It was not an ordinary beginning for the baby and his new parents, but it was certainly indicative of the lives they had led up to this point. Thomas arrived into the world in a special way, delivered by the hands of his own father.

# Chapter 23

THE FIRST MONTHS OF LITTLE Thomas's life passed more quickly than Laura would have liked. She was in a dream world. She spent most of the hours in her day holding her son, totally content to do nothing at all but stare at his little face and hold him. She sang softly to him or told him stories or played games with his little hands and feet. As he got older, she read him books and took him for long walks through the countryside in the stroller. Laura felt bad that Nick had to miss out on all the special "firsts" that Laura so eagerly reported to him when he returned home after a twelve-hour day. As Thomas quickly grew, Laura lavished attention on their son and attended to the baby's every need.

Thomas's first birthday arrived. He was already walking and into mischief. Nick and Laura held a party with all their friends and family. Aunt Gracie especially loved the child and complained on a regular basis that she was too far away from Laura and did not see him nearly enough. Laura was protective of her son and did not like traveling with him just yet.

When the baby was two years old, Nick suggested that Laura put him in a play group, or leave him with Mrs. Lafferty a few hours a day so she could get out of the house, maybe even come back to work a few days a week. Laura wouldn't even consider the possibility.

By the time Thomas turned two and a half, Laura was still insecure about doing anything out of the ordinary with her son. Her outings consisted of going shopping and going for walks, and her unhealthy aversion to traveling with her son grew. She had brought up the idea of trying for another baby, but she could sense that Nick was resistant to the idea. In the past, Laura had been adventurous. The camping and hiking she used to do became ancient history to her, and Nick had told her he thought she was shutting out a basic part of her existence. Her physical activity had been reduced to taking walks with the stroller. Nick had suggested ways to get her more involved in her own life again, but she had resisted all of them.

Finally, Nick approached Laura with an idea. He was resolved this time to get Laura to comply with him, so he used desperate tactics. A beautiful fall weekend had been forecast. Nick came home on Thursday night and made his announcement to Laura.

"Laura," he said at the dinner table that evening, "I have a surprise for you," hoping his plan would work.

"You do?" she said, picking up pieces of food that Thomas had thrown on the floor.

"Yes, I do. I've arranged to take this weekend off of work. The three of us are leaving Saturday morning for a camping trip. Isn't that wonderful?" he asked hopefully, smiling as he watched his son throw a piece of macaroni into Laura's hair.

The baby giggled, and Laura looked sternly at him and told him he'd be sitting in time-out if he threw any more food.

"Camping," she repeated, as if the word were foreign to her. "Do you really think that is a good idea? It gets pretty chilly at night this time of year."

"Yes, it does," he answered truthfully, "but we have warm clothing and a tent and sleeping bags. We will cuddle our little boy between us so he can't squirm out from under the covers, and we will get absolutely no sleep, but we will have a wonderful time."

Laura laughed at the mental picture and was pleased to see Nick smiling and happy with her response.

"Well, I guess camping might be kind of fun. I would like to go somewhere I am familiar with so there isn't any danger of getting lost or anything."

Laura had read the stories in the papers concerning the fate of Tanner Mountain. Jim's development never came to fruition, and the state had made much of the mountain into state parks, allowing those who owned it to hunt and have it preserved for their children. The thought occurred to her it would be the perfect place to camp.

Laura spent the next day packing food and equipment while Nick tied up loose ends at work. She made a trip to the grocery store and bought the necessary items, like marshmallows, Hershey bars, and graham crackers. She was actually excited about introducing her son to the delicacy of s'mores. As he ran around the store in front of the cart, much too active to remain seated in the front, she warned him not to touch anything on the shelves. She also reminisced about the sights and smells of the mountain on a crisp fall day and found herself looking forward to enjoying the weekend.

The day turned out to be sunny and gorgeous. Laura eagerly pointed out the fall foliage to her son and asked him to name all the pretty colors in the leaves. As they drove up the winding mountain roads, Laura was filled with mixed emotions. She was on edge about having her son in the woods overnight, but she could also feel a yearning to again be close to what was once a very vital part of her life. She was an experienced camper, and she tried to dispel any negative thoughts that popped into her mind. Still, there were so many dangers for a two-year-old, with the fire and putting plants in his mouth that might be poisonous. Laura told herself to chill out and that everything would be fine. *Besides,* she thought hopefully, *this may be my last chance to go camping, because by spring I hope to be pregnant again.*

Driving up a public road, they found an area that offered campsites that were fairly remote but still close enough to the road that Laura felt comfortable. She saw the rock ring that had been built by other campers that would be perfect for building their fire. They passed a Ranger station and purchased a permit for camping one night, and they received a map of the area that showed some easy trails for hiking.

Laura grew more at ease as Nick unloaded the car. Laura set Thomas loose to explore his new surroundings. He was captivated by the tiny squirrels he had discovered flitting from tree to tree. He sat down with a *thump* on his round bottom and threw tiny sticks and pebbles in the direction of the squirrels. Feeling he was in no danger, Laura decided to help Nick unload everything and set up the tent. There was a lot of work to be done, including gathering firewood. Thomas tottered around happily, amusing himself with sticks and rocks and eating the animal crackers that Laura had put in a baggie for him to snack on. He accidentally discovered that the squirrels loved them also when one dashed from behind a tree and grabbed one he had dropped a few feet behind him. Thrilled with his discovery, he squatted and watched them dart off with their treasure as he lofted animal crackers in all directions around him. Soon he had quite an assortment of friends surrounding him, and his parents watched with delight as their son experienced nature.

An hour later, the tent was up, and Laura was pounding the last of the tent stakes securely in the ground with a large rock, since Nick had forgotten the hammer. Laura was enjoying the physical activity. Thomas made a game of running in and out of the tent and was absolutely thrilled that this was where he was going to be sleeping.

Dusk would be setting in shortly when Nick announced that he was going to look for some firewood. The days were becoming shorter, and Laura couldn't believe this one was almost over already. They would do their hiking tomorrow. As she pounded stakes in the last side of the tent, from behind her she heard Nick say that he was going to look for wood and that he would take Thomas with him. Laura yelled, "Okay," as she continued to pound.

Laura started to get concerned that Nick and Thomas hadn't returned. She listened carefully and could hear the distant sound of Nick's ax chopping a tree. She had to laugh at his over exuberance and wondered how he was going to cart back all the wood he had been chopping out there. She could picture him walking back through the woods with his arms full of wood, her tiny son toddling behind him carrying one or two sticks, thinking he was Daddy's big helper.

The evening air was even chillier than she had expected, and she wished Nick would hurry up with the wood so she could get the fire started. Thomas had only a thin jacket on because the day had been so warm earlier. Going into the tent, she pulled on a thick sweater and grabbed a jacket for Thomas. She decided to go meet them in the woods.

Suddenly she had a bad feeling in the pit of her stomach, a hunch, a mother's instinct. She recalled the moment Nick had left her to go get wood. It had not occurred to her before that she might have mistaken what he said to her because of the noise she was making pounding the stakes. It just didn't make sense for Nick to be taking the baby to chop wood, though. *Nick* did *say he was taking Thomas with him, didn't he?* Terror gripped her as she slipped into the woods, homing in on the sound of Nick's ax. She ran through the woods with the agility and quickness of a deer. In no time she found Nick. He stood, staring at the shocked look on her face when she burst in front of him, without Thomas in tow.

"What's the matter?" he asked with concern, the ax slipping from his hand.

"Where is the baby? Nick, please tell me you know where he is!" she said, her eyes frantically searched the area around them.

"I told you I was leaving him with you, and you said okay," Nick shouted angrily.

"I didn't hear you right. I thought you said you were taking him with you," she shouted back.

"Why would I take my baby son to chop wood?" he yelled.

Both of them were starting to panic.

"Oh my God," Laura gasped, finally giving in to her fear. She turned and fled into the woods, screaming her son's name.

"*Thomas! Where are you, baby? Thomas, come to Mommy!*" she screamed.

Nick took off in a different direction, calling out the boy's name as he ran. He felt the darkness closing in, almost suffocating him. He also noticed as he called his son's name that plumes of white followed his words, indicating that the temperature was quickly dropping.

They searched the immediate area until it was totally dark. The moon was hidden from them behind a thick bank of clouds, and the woods were cloaked in black. Laura lay in a heap by the edge of the woods, sobbing for her lost son, unable to yell any longer because she had lost her voice.

Finally Nick got in the car and drove back to the Ranger station to get help. Laura sat up as headlights flashed across her, indicating that Nick had returned, with help, she hoped. She was relieved to see two men pull up in a jeep behind Nick and jump out of the car.

Laura and Nick gave the men the exact details of the situation. They tried to remain as unemotional as possible in order to ensure they gave the correct information. One of the men returned to his jeep and used the radio to gather more help to form a search party.

An additional hour went by before the men arrived. Laura and Nick both wanted to go out on their own rather than sit and wait for help to arrive. It tore Laura's heart to think of her child alone, lost in the dark woods. He was probably huddled somewhere, freezing and hungry. Flashbacks of her own childhood invaded her thoughts, and she went into a trance, remembering huddling in her own dark places, leaves drawn around her for warmth. But she had been ten, Thomas was only two. He was so little and vulnerable.

Nick had to shake Laura to bring her back to reality. "The men are here with lots of help. We are going to organize this search and bring home our baby," Nick told her, hugging her tightly.

The group had brought maps, and quadrants were sectioned off, a pair of people responsible for searching each one. They all realized the necessity of finding the child as soon as possible because of the dropping temperatures, though the volunteers avoided being too blunt and upsetting the parents even more than they already were.

Each parent paired with a Ranger. Laura and Nick and the rest of the group set off at slight angles to one another to begin the search. Well after midnight, the groups filtered back to the tent site; there'd been no signs of the boy. Nick and Laura's groups were the last to return. Exhausted, Laura dropped next to the fire that one of the first returning parties had built. Someone placed a blanket over her shoulders as she sat crying, arms crossed over her knees, rocking and sobbing. Nick sat next to her, crying silent tears. He looked at the few night stars peeking between the clouds that dotted the sky and watched his wife as she suffered through the heartache, her heart ripping to pieces over the loss of her son.

A few of the cars departed. The head Ranger walked over to the fire and knelt down between Laura and Nick.

"We covered as much terrain as possible in the dark. We are going to resume the search at first light. That's in only a few hours. We are going to find your son in the morning. Keep faith. I will be back before the crack of dawn."

Nick had to half carry Laura into the tent. Her body temperature was dropping, and he had to force her into the down sleeping bag. Nick closed his eyes and moved as close to Laura as possible and tried to get some sleep.

Laura returned to a trancelike state. She had once been in a state similar to this one, but her mind did not remember that now. She was in so much mental agony that her spirit wanted to leave her body behind and go away to a place that offered her peace and warmth. But something once again held her back. It was not her time to leave just yet. A familiar sensation overcame her; she felt herself hovering outside her own body. She could sense, not see, Nick lying beside her. She could feel his pain as well as her own.

Suddenly, she felt herself being carried out of the tent and away from the campsite. She was flying across the tops of the trees effortlessly. The night was dark, but she could sense that she was being drawn to some specific place by some specific force. Her journey was not as far as it was the first time she had the experience. She arrived at a rocky ledge hidden in a thick group of trees that seemed to surround it in a protective circle. Within the circle of trees, deep beneath the ledge, was a familiar place. Laura could sense that this was a place often visited by someone she knew. Through that entity, she could feel the contours of the floor and sense the closeness of the rocky ledge above her head. There were small bones scattered around the floor of the area. She could sense that there was something different about the place this evening. An unfamiliar presence was there, a presence that needed protecting. It was an unfamiliar but strangely familiar presence all the same. She could feel the entity wrapping itself around the presence and using the warmth of its body to shelter it from the cold. The presence made strange noises that were again familiar but strange, all at the same time. Laura observed the situation in a detached manner, but the vision brought a peace to her that she would not remember when she woke, long before the first light of dawn.

Laura woke before Nick. She heard a car pull up and then another and realized that dawn must be near. She left her sleeping bag and walked out of the tent. She began to stoke the fire, bringing the dying embers back to life.

Nick rolled over. Not finding Laura next to him, he popped out of the tent to find her. She was standing by the fire lost in thought. Nick walked up behind her and placed his hand on her shoulder. Without words, she let him know that she would accept his love and not turn away in anger or blame him for the terrible situation they were now facing. She simply placed her hand on top of his. She felt his arm and hand relax as he drew in a deep breath. He wrapped his arms around her from behind and hugged her tightly. Someone brought them steaming cups of coffee, which they accepted gratefully. They waited for the search party to arrive.

As the first rays of dawn lit the horizon with a pinkish hue, the teams once again set out to find Thomas. This time, several of the parties brought search-and-rescue dogs. Laura teared up as she handed a tiny sock, sweater, and pair of jeans to the searchers for the dogs to sniff for Thomas's scent. It broke her heart not to have her son there with her, to be able to dress him, hold him, and keep him warm. The dogs barked excitedly and pulled on their leashes. The lead dog seemed to pick up a scent immediately. It pulled at the leash, sniffing the ground furiously. Laura and Nick followed hopefully. The animal seemed possessed, intent on finding his quarry. Setting a quick pace, the animal lost the scent a couple of times but eventually decided on a fresh trail. Each time the dog paused, Laura's hopes would drop, sending her on a roller coaster of emotions.

Suddenly, the dog barked and raced ahead as fast as his handler would allow. After a half a mile or so, the dog began to slow and seemed to become confused again. Laura had begun to lose faith that the dog was actually following her son's scent, when up ahead, she saw a familiar ring of trees. She didn't know why they were familiar; she didn't recall seeing them the day before. All of a sudden, the dog stopped dead still, and the hairs on his neck bristled. A deep growl emanated from his throat. Laura had the frightening feeling the dog had been following the wrong trail and had led them to something dangerous.

"What's going on?" Nick asked the dog handler.

"I don't know. I have no idea why he is afraid," the handler answered.

Laura could tell the dog handler was confused by the dog's reaction, but Laura had a strange feeling, and she couldn't quite figure out where the feeling was coming from. The dog wouldn't move forward, so Laura passed him. She stopped and checked her surroundings. Her instincts told her there was no dangerous predator around, or all the dogs would have been here, barking furiously. She crept cautiously forward, resolved to follow her instincts.

"Wait. Stop! We don't know what's in there," the handler warned as he saw Laura crouch and begin looking into the underbrush.

Nick held up a hand and told the handler, "It's okay. Trust me; she knows what she's doing."

The dog handler shrugged and put a consoling hand on the dog's broad shoulders; it stood still, tense and growling.

Nick caught up with Laura, trailing closely behind her as she moved forward to investigate the area.

Laura felt as if she were being drawn forward, almost in a trance, oblivious to the world around her. She found a trail leading into the thicket that became almost like a low tunnel, only a few feet high. Crawling on hands and knees, Nick right behind her, she crept into the brush. She discovered that it opened to a clearing in the middle of the ring of trees, and dead center was a rock ledge. All of a sudden, Laura and Nick heard a sound—a giggle. It was a wonderful, familiar, happy laugh that neither one of them could mistake. Almost running over one another, they climbed around the ledge and peered under the overhang. What they encountered was a sight that would forever be etched in both of their memories.

The search dog relaxed when the humans disappeared into the brush. The danger he sensed, the mixture of the scents that had confused him, no longer frightened him. Behind him, other dogs were barking, and a few teams converged to find the dog handler standing and staring into the brush.

"What did you find, Hank?" one of the other dog handlers asked. He held his dog back from charging into the underbrush.

"I don't know. Things got kind of strange for a second, and the parents just disappeared into that brush. Sinbad here smelled something he didn't like, but they seemed to want to check it out anyway," he told the others.

Each of the dogs was now wriggling with excitement, pulling at the leashes to follow their quarry into the thicket. The dog handlers and other members of the search party hovered around, not sure what to think of the situation.

As Nick and Laura bent down and looked under the ledge, the heaviness and despair that they had felt for all those long hours melted away instantly. Their son, filthy but obviously healthy and unharmed, lay with his arms wrapped around the neck of a huge golden retriever. Laura and Nick gasped in disbelief.

"Momma!" Thomas cried out with glee. He sprang up from the dog and tottered into his mother's arms.

The dog stood, barely enough room for his head under the shelf, and Laura and he locked eyes in a familiar stare.

"You are not going to believe this, Nick!" she cried to her husband, who wrapped his son with his arms and hugged him tightly. "I know this dog." Through tears of joy, Laura managed a formal introduction. "Nick, meet Alex. Alex, meet Nick."

At the sound of his name, Alex came bounding out of the cave and licked Laura's face, remembering instantly her smell and the sound of her voice. She burrowed her face into his thick coat and hugged him fiercely.

Laura looked at Nick; he was speechless with amazement. Laura could not believe after all these years, after surviving alone in the woods, the dog still remembered her. Not only did he remember her, but he'd saved her son's life. Sensing a familiar presence in the boy, the dog had enough sense to bring the child to his shelter and protect him with the heat of his body.

Cradling his son in his arms, Nick reached over and petted the dog's thick golden fur. The dog turned to face him, and their eyes locked. Laura smiled through her tears and reached over once again to hug her son, her husband, and the animal that had saved her son's life.


"What the heck do you think they are doing in there?" one man said, nervous that the couple had not yet emerged.

To the shock and surprise of the search party, a large yellow dog bounded out of the thicket. He wagged his tail. The group of search dogs sniffed cautiously at the new canine; some issued warning growls. Others warmed up more quickly to the outsider. Then Nick and Laura crawled through the bushes, trailing after their son.

Cheers and shouts filled the forest as relief and joy filled the hearts of the searchers. The dogs began barking, sensing the humans were excited and happy. Thomas was passed from person to person. Each Ranger and searcher had to hug him and feel for themselves that he was alive and well.

One of the Rangers, hearing the story of how Nick and Laura had discovered the boy, admitted that he had heard rumors about a large yellow dog wandering the area. A few campers had reported that a big dog had snuck into their campsites and stolen steaks and hamburgers right off the grill. They had never been able to catch the bandit. Laura was sure glad they never had.

The crew of searchers, happy parents, and the sleepy, hungry little boy emerged from the woods to be greeted by several reporters and news cameras. Word of the lost boy and the search for him had spread like wildfire through the media. They had finally pinpointed the location of the scene where all the action was taking place.

Nick and Laura stood close together, son in Nick's arms and dog by Laura's side, trying to be polite but obviously eager to be on their way, answering only a few questions while cameras flashed and the news reporters zoomed in on each of the characters in the story. A Ranger finally stepped in and asked everyone to respect their privacy and let them get their little boy home. He ushered the family to their car and assured them he would pack up all their belongings and keep them at the station until they could return and pick everything up. Medics, who had been called to the scene when the news spread that the child had been found, offered to take Thomas to the hospital and have him checked out. Both Nick and Laura declined, sensing that all their little boy needed was to be home with them, safe and sound.

The Jacksons returned home that afternoon with a new addition to their family. On the return trip, Laura sat in the backseat, nestled between the baby and the dog, and felt that even though there had been a near tragedy that weekend, there had also been great fortune. She felt alive and herself again; an uncompleted circle in her life had been reconnected, and everything was right in the world. The next time the family went camping, she was definitely going to bring the dog.

CPSIA information can be obtained at www.ICGtesting.com
Printed in the USA
BVOW03s1949290713

327231BV00002B/173/P